The Adventures of Tina and Randy

The Parlor, The Iron, and The Pilot

Richard A. Boehler, Jr.

authorHOUSE®

AuthorHouse™
1663 Liberty Drive
Bloomington, IN 47403
www.authorhouse.com
Phone: 833-262-8899

Published by AuthorHouse 09/22/2022

ISBN: 978-1-6655-7131-9 (sc)
ISBN: 978-1-6655-7132-6 (e)

Print information available on the last page.

Contents

The Parlor

The Iron

The Pilot's Story

The Parlor

Richard Alexander Boehler, Jr.

Chapter 1

It was early evening when Randy entered the gym. At the front desk, a tall lady greeted people as they showed their membership cards. She was the owner. A nice lady, that recently bought the gym. She had retired from a basketball career, due to a severe ankle injury. Randy entered, smiled at the nice lady, then made his way to the locker room. It was a small gym. Not too much bigger than the high school weight room. It was designed well. There was a separate room where cardio equipment was placed. A separated room where boxing equipment could be found. A guys and ladies locker room – with showers and bathrooms. The biggest room was just past all this. And, in that room of the gym was the universal weight machines, squat racks, bench presses and bar bells..., along with a good amount of dumb bells. All the things needed to get fit! Of course, there was music too! The cost of the membership was monthly. Most gyms operate that way. Back then, the membership was approximately seventeen bucks a month. Not too bad for a private gym. It was more though. It was a home away from home…. [sometimes in this life, that home away from "home" is necessary, is good, is a tool for survival…]. Randy was young – a freshman in college (18 years). He liked to exercise…. It was good for the heart, good for the appetite/digestion/et cetera. And he liked to build muscle.

The weight room is where Randy spent most of his time. He was stocky, big…. But, not too big. At least most wouldn't know it with a quick glance at him. He thought that it was sort of like meeting an elite warrior in the armed forces. For example, an army ranger or a Navy Seal. At first glance, most would not know what the musculature, the tissues, the organs, the anatomy and physiology were really trained to do, was trained to handle; what was trained with the most extreme conditions… Randy just enjoyed the fitness though. It was something to grow into, to build into, and develop. Shifting exercise regiments was key too. Bouncing between the weights and the cardio exercises was always a good approach. And that is where he met Tina.... Tina, and her friend. Her friend did not like him, and he never understood why that was.... Later, he found that she labelled him as a gym player! ... Randy thought that was so ironic – most people do, in fact, judge a book by its cover... and for people that was no exception.... He was used to that... and smiled because it could not be furthest from the truth.... It wasn't him – he was not that type of guy... not that it didn't cross his mind to be that way... it was just, deep inside, the moral compass was something fierce, something strong... he was always that relationship type, the family man type... and that was good with him... it was the way he was designed, and that was something he knew could not be "faked..." that was just there or it wasn't there...

Randy needed to laminate his new gym card, and so he decided to go back to the front of the gym to pick up his fresh card. At the front of the gym stood two ladies. They were paying their monthly gym fee and giggling…. They were obviously friends. Randy introduced himself and started flirting with the cute Italian lady. She was athletic strong with Italian qualities. Her name was Tina. Tina's friend did not like him, much…. That was okay, not everyone is a fan… anyway…. They "clicked".

The town was a modest, small suburban town – located far out into the Atlantic-ocean…. In fact, it was called an island, "long island". Travel to this town was simple, but took time…. A straight road that ran across west to east brought the traveler to the main island. About two hours into the drive, and further out into the Atlantic ocean – Randy and Tina lived. Well, the town was not on the main part of the island. A ferry ride was needed. Just north of the "main island" was a small deserted island, where they lived….

The gym was the "local gym", where everyone went. That is… "everyone" was all the people they knew at the time! It was "their world". And that world was "huge"! (so they thought… at that point in time….) It is fascinating, looking back on things… The world in this small town did, in fact, seem like the biggest world they knew! Of course, that was not true... and Randy sort of knew that (in that point in time...) - not that he understood what that meant.... Deep inside him, a flame burned that directed a compass.... The compass was kind of passed on through evolutionary mechanisms... which he did not fully understand (in that point in time). It was a good thing though (he thought...). A feeling of "manifest destiny". Perhaps, that was the energy that made "America"; the America we all knew. The feeling of the pursuit of "something". For Randy and he would soon realize.... For Tina too, that the feeling was mutual, the feeling to pursue something! The pursuit of adventure! This energy is not shared by everyone, and that is what differentiated some from others, and others from some.... Randy smiled! It was true, and it was not that he did not "appreciate" the most conservative life. He did and he "visited" that life... when he could. (He thought, and smiled). Tina was the same way! And he loved that about her. Meeting her parents was... "interesting". You see, her father was co-owner of the local funeral parlor. They say hindsight is 20/20. And that is true. At the time, he just thought it was... "different", cool... he guessed (thinking).... But, did not have too much time to ponder while eating dinner because her parents were "social", were "inviting, entertaining", and could tell a great story! Before he could give the funeral parlor another thought, her parents remarked that the china they were eating dinner on was from a recent trip they had taken.... Randy was intrigued.... They visited France! He loved that, since he knew some of the French language (he spoke the greetings and was capable of ordering cheese, bread and coca cola.... Ya know, all the things needed to survive in France!).

While they ate, the phones rang off the hook! Her father did not answer, but the voice mail could clearly be heard! It was a message for another death. The funeral arrangements needed to be made as soon as possible. There was a process to this. So, her father left dinner to call back and make arrangements... After dinner, Tina and Randy took a drive. Tina wanted to show Randy something.... He was curious. What she wanted to, what she needed to show him... was... "The parlor" (Randy breathed deep, and was questioned by Tina!). He laughed, and stated that he thought she meant something else, when she said "she wanted to show him something". They laughed, together – as their eyes met and lock!

The parlor was dark. All the lights were turned off. She brought a good flash light. They entered with the key she had on her car key ring…. Inside, it was even darker. The flashlight provided some glow directly in front of them… as they opened the cellar door to start the step by step decent into the basement… down in the cellar, the smell of chemicals to embalm the dead was evident. Tina led the way as Randy followed. She quickly turned her head back to Randy and smirked… "smells funny", doesn't it? Randy giggled, awkwardly! They continued to walk through the basement, right alongside a dead body and to the back of the room… far, in the back corner of the dark basement was a desk and chairs. They sat. Tina motioned to Randy, pointing to the first seat across from the desk. She sat behind the desk, with her feet up. Randy asked what they were doing. Tina let a long pause of silence pass…. Seemed like a good five minutes…. Then she smiled and said "welcome to my office", would we be doing business tonight? She laughed, burst out into laughter – she could not keep a straight face. Perhaps, it was the dead body located directly behind Randy.... Perhaps it was just his silly expression (a sort of frightened bewildered look) but, randy surprised Tina. He was more comfortable, then she realized! he began conversation with a genuine interest in her, an honest approach to what he called "courtship". She hadn't met a guy like Randy before.... And he admitted, that he was a "rare breed" (to this day, he wasn't sure if that was a good or a bad thing.... He hoped it was a good thing for her). In the dark, they sat there – giggling and locked eyes .... They knew that there was something between them.... Because, you see.... She was a rare breed to! Randy called her an angel.... He could see the shine in her eyes (for one thing...) and he just felt the connection. It was faster than a heartbeat.... The connection between Tina and Randy was quicker than the electrical signal through a myelinated sheath of human nerves (...that transfer of electrical signaling from the brain to muscle and back to the brain.... That is pretty damn fast!). A connection that was unique/rare/special in nature! The synergistic connection of Tina and Randy's heart, mind, body, souls – they shared this feeling, it was heaven on earth (and Randy thought, without any doubt that A. she was an angel and B. they were soulmates!).

The cellar was no ordinary basement design…. It seemed more like a research laboratory, minus the one dead body. The capacity of the cellar area could hold six to seven dead bodies (if it needed to). Tina explained the lab, she stopped… and giggled…. "The parlor's purpose". Randy looked at her, in suspect. Was this "parlor" really an area for dead body preparation? He thought that it might be there for some other purpose. Perhaps a front to something other than parlor services…. The design did seem odd. It wasn't "make-shift". There were clear areas of the space that seemed to have been designed for certain tasks. Behind Tina, the book shelf had hundreds of manuals. Manuals that were instructions for embalming bodies with chemicals?

They talked for a while. Randy thought that the parlor business wasn't a common business to be in. Not that it wasn't needed. Sure, it was needed. He had never been so close to corpses, never this close. He dissected some things in school... a sheep's eye, a pig, a dog-shark, a brain, heart and a cat. To be this close to a rotting corpse seemed... like he was in a horror movie. So, they decided to call it a night... As they walked up the cellar steps, two things struck Randy's attention. The first was that he thought the place the corpse had been in... moved! The body did not seem to have been in the same spot.... Then he thought that there was no way a corpse could move from one area to the next.... The corpse was rotting... that would be impossible! The second, was a bright red glow. It was quick, similar to the glow that is seen in a cat's eye – if the night hits it right.... Tina was not a cat, though. Randy looked closer at her, but it happened too fast. A reflective light from her eye! They closed the cellar door, then left the parlor...

It certainly was a fascinating night. [as they drove back to her parent's house, Randy thought that she was very unique – different. It seemed she took a liking to the "dark arts". Or maybe it was just that it was the "family business" – the upkeep and maintenance of the local town parlor.... Randy wasn't sure what to think of it, yet. At that moment in time, it seemed (to him) ... to be fascinating, and he smiled at Tina.]

Tina drove a pretty nice car for the rural, no name Long Island Town.... Located adrift, off the coast of eastern long island (somewhere out into the Atlantic-ocean). The car was "luxury" compared to local standards. And Randy knew it, as soon as he sat down in the passenger seat – that cool autumn evening. Tina powered the radio, turned on some hip-hop music tunes and asked Randy if he wanted the seat warmer on. He did and they talked during the ride back to her place. She was an adventurous type; Randy liked that. She loved sports. A good quality to add (in his opinion). Not just the fascination with dark arts, but she was also a pretty good boxing light weight! They spent time together, in the gym. And, usually met in the cardio room for stair stepper competitions, followed by a good session of boxing. She wasn't that bad an athlete! At her home, she showed him a secret room. It was sort of a "chamber", where files upon files were kept. The files were of human corpses (some went as far back as fifty years!). Tina pulled a file and showed the detailed color photos. The wounds (if there were any), the process of getting bodies ready for final funeral arrangements, etc. [again, Randy thought he had never been so close to a rotting corpse before…. It was … fascinating, he smiled then frowned in an awkward way].

The "business" was more than parlor tricks. There was something else happening. Tina was friendly and excited to talk about the "after life". It seemed as if she knew a lot about the "after life". The parent's left for the evening to see a movie. That left Tina and Randy alone in the house. They decided to pop some popcorn, and watch a video. By the time her parents arrived home – they found Tina with Randy, asleep in the den. The movie had ended…. They looked like two peas in a pod… so, Tina's parents decided to let them be for the evening….

The next morning, was the weekend. Randy woke to a great breakfast that had been cooked. This was exciting, since he usually was the type always on the go… eating as he traveled…. A home cooked breakfast was awesome. Actually, he thought any home cooked meal was awesome! (his child upbringing consisted of pot luck dinners and other meals... not much family time at a table with a nicely cooked meal.... Holidays were always pretty good though, his mom made up for all the time lost during the holiday meal preps!). This was nice... to see people at their finest, in the morning. No masks! It was real "family" conversations. Coming from a big family, there was never a dull moment... no cutting corners on the drama, coming from a big family! Tina's family was smaller, and very formal.... He liked it... they were down to earth (or what some would say, hospitable...), he liked that too....

The family had plans for the weekend, and Randy needed to head back to the University... to catch up on some stuff. Tina asked her family if she could skip the plans to join Randy at University. Looking at these two... they were two peas in a pod. Her family could not object, they were happy! Randy was excited too. He wanted to show her some things in the University research laboratory....

Chapter 2

The trip up to "University" was quick. Usually, the drive took about thirty minutes from where they lived, minus the ferry ride off the island. Approaching the campus, it seemed to swell into another world. The grounds were filled with many trees – forest like. Close to nature. The main entrance was gated, but was usually open to students, staff and visitors... Overnight, main entry gates were closed and only a few of the side gates remained open, with a police presence. Tina parked her car in one of the student lots... Randy had a card that was placed on the car dash board. Of course, even with this card, he found himself with good amounts of parking tickets, each semester. Twenty-five bucks each ticket wasn't too bad, for a University setting. Parking in areas close to the lecture halls was typically reserved for VP level people. Running late for class prompted Randy to take evasive action – sometimes...

The walk from the car parking lot to the research laboratory was a good half hour! The campus had open space, acres upon acres of "forest", with winding trails for bicycling and walking.... Sometimes they liked to mountain bike the trails, through the campus – together. Other times, it was just as nice to take a stroll along the paths – drinking a hot cup of Starbucks coffee.... The morning was brisk, with the cool breezes coming off the not to distant body of water – the Long Island Sound. As they walked, they sipped fresh coffee – light and sweet! The biology building was a mini skyscraper, right on campus grounds. It was surprising to see, compared to the other University architecture... Most buildings were one to three stories in height. This biology research building was hidden. Deep in the forest, back from the lecture halls. Back from the dorms. Back from the student activity centers, where a good selection of food could be found. Tina and Randy entered the main lobby with an electronic access card. In the lobby, the design was simple and amazing.

Like walking back to prehistoric times. The plants were robust and everywhere, from wall to wall – up to the ceiling and around the halls…. The oxygen content of the lobby also seemed different. There was an obvious increase in the amount of oxygen to breath… plant photosynthesis at its best! They smiled at each other…. Then entered the stair well, to descend into a basement laboratory. Although, this was nothing like the parlor basement. It was just an entryway to another area. They entered an elevator at that point, which subsequently brought them deep into the earth… a good twenty-minute journey….

The light in the secret place was phenomenal! It was not a dreary basement at all. In fact, there were corridors dedicated to different areas of scientific research. Randy's friend came over to introduce his area. His studies were in the field of entomology, insects. But, not just the insect species along the south American coast line…. The rain forest plants too! The entry way into his lab was tight. It was a gowning air lock – without the gowning! The airlock could hold a group of people, it closed and sprayed a violent force of disinfectant spray over their clothes and bodies, that quickly dried. The next room was a locker room, where they changed out of their street clothes – into comfy jump suits....

The main laboratory was essentially an indoor green house, with various species of dense plant life, trees – with immense canopies. The ceiling was high and the forest was similar to a real rain forest! They could not tell the difference between the two forests; natural verse basement natural! It truly was an amazing lab. Tina and Randy followed "Chuck" through the vegetation – and eventually made their way to his desk. Funny thing, a forest at the bottom of this biological life science building... and deep into the forest was a nice marbled desk, with computer, phone line, a "Zen" sand garden on top of the desk, a nice leather chair, and a group of visitor chairs. Chuck sat behind the desk and invited Tina to sit with Randy in the other chairs. As they were looking around, into the deep forest – chuck opened a program on his computer to initiate a two phased approach to office perimeter fencing. When activated, an invisible laser fence appeared (sort of, only seen if they looked close at a red beamed circumference). The second phase opened a bunker. The bunker led to an underground sleeping facility, complete with an entertainment room, showers and a kitchen. Chuck explained the purpose of the phased fencing and living quarters. The experiments lasted weeks into the month time line....

He was protected from the elements outside the fencing. Tina stopped him and asked why he was worried about the elements in the forest... wasn't this just entomology? What kind of insects were you breeding? Chuck smirked and giggled, awkwardly... then looked over at Randy. Randy chimed in.... There was more to the experiments. There were multiple, very diverse experiments being performed in different areas of science. Chuck liked the insects and the plants.... Randy did too! But, he smirked back at Chuck, then paused... for a long time.... Followed with a brief summary of his interests.... You see, my interests are more "pragmatic". Tina was curious, asking what he meant by the word "pragmatic". Randy cackled... in a strange way... but, she thought it was cute.... He intrigued her... and when he summarized his interest in applying the plant life species (rare species) with the insect species (rare species) to human cellular systems…. Her eyebrows raised! She stopped them… and asked, are you suggesting that there is some way to bring back the dead?

The biology of a living system was absolutely intriguing, fascinating, complex in so many ways. There two ways to approach it, though. To sort of, organize it – in a more manageable way. Which, ultimately simplified the complexity of it. If that were even possible. At least, if not simplify the complexity of biological systems…. It certainly placed it into clear cut groups….so that it was more "understandable". The two areas were (A) anatomy and (B) physiology. And within A and B, there was further organization, simplification… The group talked for a while, and toured the living areas. Chuck presented some of his findings, preliminary stuff…then advised that they leave the laboratory (his area, anyway). He needed to secure the perimeters, and ensure that no one was taking any stroll through the forest… it could be dangerous.

As they left the biology facility, for the day – Tina wondered what was so dangerous in that man made forest? There was more to the story, she knew it and she was going to find out…. Randy and Tina made their way to his dorm to take a quick nap; just after picking up some Chinese cuisine from the on-campus food court…. Time flies when you're having fun. And they were in love. Having the time of their lives. It was fascinating, really. It was almost as if the laws of time did not apply to them…. And perhaps there was some truth to that…. The circle of love was a special circle, with an incredible level of happiness. Not that there were no ripples within the circle, there were. After all, she was a fisty type personality…. A spark…. To speak to it in a kind way…. The personality was cute to Randy. He couldn't imagine a more perfect combination of cuteness, fashion, mixed in with electricity! Just perfect…. He was learning her ways…. The funny thing, though… was that she was also learning his ways…. His "other-life" (as he sometimes referred to it) was not such a bland, dull life…. Randy appreciated peace and serenity, but the "other life" was also a part of his inner self…. The experience of chugging beer and finding the party.... His style had always been a more conservative approach.... Even in the "other life". And that was perfectly okay with him... as long as there was some beer there. These days, he had an appreciation for a good baseball game, a good movie and good food... a more "family oriented" conservative guy he evolved into.... Somewhere along the way...

The inner sense of adventure was always there. So, while the children in the dorms were playing loud music, smoking things, drinking lots of alcohol and slamming walls for fun.... Randy left with Tina.... It was late night now. They had discussed "the adventure" that was needed. The "mission" was simple. Pack a bag with the essentials: protein bars and water...some snacks.... Then get into the basement forest lab....to see what the hell was really going on down there...! Access into the biological science building was easy. Randy had an electronic card to enter the lobby. Some of the students had late night classes, or were carrying out the experiments to support various class curriculum. In the basement was the problem. They could not access the forest lab, the door was locked. Tina surprised Randy when she picked the lock! Within five minutes, they were standing at the edge of the "man-made" forest. The strange thing was that it seemed to be no different from being in a south American rain forest! In the essential back pack, Randy pulled out a map and a compass. And one other, very important thing – a pretty good flash light! They were going to need it. And as they walked straight into the forest, the surroundings got dark – pitch black! More disturbing, though, was the sound in the distance. A beast like sound. They wondered….

Luckily, Tina found the trail that brought them near the research pod. They recognized it immediately! The main computer-controlled a perimeter, a circle that covered the area surrounding the research pod. Tina activated the perimeter fence, which must have had some sort of invisible laser to the mechanism…. Once all the lights on the computer console lit bright orange, they felt better. The sounds in the distance, were not as concerning to them… (not that they wanted the beast making the sound to test the perimeter fencing… they did not). It was very late, and walking through the dense forest in the dark tired them... Tina opened the door to the pod, and signaled Randy to follow her inside. The interior living space was modern in style. Although, it was also similar to an open spaced laboratory. The living area had some basic furniture, consisting of couches and an entertainment area (television, movies, etc.). The kitchen was simple, but had a good refrigerator and stove for cooking/storage of food. The Pod was good square footage, and led to an elevator. The elevator brought Tina and Randy into the main research operations area. It reminded Tina of the parlor basement....

Inside the "living quarters" was a laboratory. The manuals Tina found on the desk shelf detailed the research experiments being performed in the forest. The hypothesis was straight forward: inclusion of plant matter, electricity and some sort of "ritual" enabled the dead to become "living". Biological systems were complex, and the systems required certain nutrients to maintain "life". When the nutrients stopped or a significant disruption of the system occurred, life no longer existed.... These research papers outlined the subject, using various life forms.... Animals and even some dead human bodies! Fascinating, Tina yelled out.... Randy was not so sure that the "experiments" were so "fascinating". He started wondering about the strange animal like howls in the dark forest.... Tina smirked, as she continued to read the literature....

There were contacts listed on a sheet of paper, this grabbed Randy's attention. The contact was a local town mechanic. What was strange with the list....as Randy read it.... Was the fact that "people" listed on this list was recently also listed in the local town obituaries! Tina knew the mechanic. He recently had worked on her car. Randy paused and was quiet for what seemed an eternity. Tina nudged him, then kissed his cheek. He was startled.... then spoke. Remember the story I told you about the Washington Bridge? You know, the GWB? With my car? This guy had also worked on my car.... And one night, driving across the GWB – to get back onto Long Island.... My brakes went! No brakes, traveling about fifty miles an hour....! Crazy, right? Randy breathed a sigh of relief.... "Thank goodness for some very relevant training...". In the madness, he kept calm and softly applied the emergency level.... The car slowed... then, he drove it that way... back home! The thing is, this mechanic seemed to have some link to these people.... The "recently deceased" (he should say...).

There was silence... and a look of concern on both their faces. It was in that moment that they knew, something sinister was happening here. The howl outside the perimeter seemed to be louder. Seemed to be getting "closer". Tina photo copied the list and some other technical documents... it just seemed odd to have this kind of literature in a "forest". The technicality of it delved into genetics, anatomy, physiology, cell surface biology and cellular signaling. More scope then was typical for the study of plants, herbs and some wild life. Tina copied some of the technical literature. There were human cells in the body. In fact, that's just what we are made of! Trillions of cells. Not just a single cell. Groups of cells that are organized into higher leveled functional components: tissues, organs, systems...it is fascinating! So, what happens when a critical system stops working? Life ends. Life here! There is certainly more to it, more than just structure. It is the way it all functions – the physiological pathways...the fuel of most of each system is an internal transfer of nutrients, that keep a constant charge of energy – electricity! Tina joked: maybe Mary Shelly wasn't to far from reality, when she wrote the book "Frankenstein"! Something was happening here. More than just simple jungle experiments... there was bursting sound, just outside the building! Followed with a scratching sound.... Similar to metal nails on iron walls.... The sound suddenly ended. Tina and Randy looked up at each other!

They found the documents they needed to find. They copied what they could... then decided it was time to go. Randy and Tina left the jungle quietly and cautiously.... And in the distance, the howl of animals was evident. The campus was calm and peaceful, while they strolled the paths, leading back to

Randy's dorm. Of course, on the way – they picked up a snack and some fresh coffee. In the still of the night, they talked…. Enjoyed the coffee and really took a liking to the company. She was brilliant and feisty…. Randy liked that about Tina. Just perfect… well, not perfect… which (in his mind) was… "perfect". The night was serene, a pristine glow of the moon completed what would be a very nice piece of art (Randy explained to Tina, his interest in various hobbies…. It wasn't the science, only, that intrigued him… it was "being cultured"). Learning more of art – especially landscape are, impressionistic styled art – where colors were blended into various scenes…. The culture of music; many different types of music…. Everything from Baroque (1300s) into the birth of Rock and Roll (1950s), into the hard rock of the 1970, with 80s style and his personal favorite: the 1990s! (Alternative, grunge, alternative-rock styles of music genres).

They were growing to be a pretty good couple. It was nice, the conversation… the coffee, and the moonlight…. Randy wanted to know more about Tina. (He thought he knew a lot, but wasn't that kind of the way of a relationship? The building, where over time he would learn more...). Tina talked of her interest in art, music, fashion... and as she continued to talk.... The calmness of her voice sedated Randy.... Together, they fell asleep somewhere – someplace (in her cute conversation). The next morning, they found themselves starting a weekend together! It was absolutely breathtaking! To start a Saturday morning with the right lady, the right sort of people! (The magic of soul mates...). They agreed to jog 20 to 40 minutes – and that is what they did! The jog was paced, and that was okay with Randy... he could push a sprint... but the way he evaluated the "strategy of the run", was to set goals.... Perhaps, incorporate some "sprint" within the paced jog. Perhaps, incorporate some "incline" within the paced jog.... There were different scenarios. Today, they kept it to a paced jog – with some inclines along the way. The air was crisp and cool – great for this time of year (autumn).... Afterwards, they showered – together. Nothing sexual, but certainly a shower that depicted the love they showed for one another.... Her hair was gorgeous, all the hair she showed was like a drug to Randy... he was addicted to her hair.... (Which, fascinated him, intrigued him.... Sparked a curiosity within him, to understand what in the world was so special about her hair? He didn't know, not yet.... He wanted to find out though? The answer could not be written or spoken... it was felt, in the connection between Tina and Randy's hearts! Their souls....

Breakfast consisted of toasted bagels (sesame seed) and the fresh coffee! Tina was concerned about the "mechanic". Randy was too! Something was not right in their local no name town... on an island, away from "the real world". On that island, they suspected that the "mechanic" was targeting people, murdering the targets and transferring the dead bodies to the "biological science building", right on campus – in the "jungle", that they had just returned from...They were not sure what to do about it. So, they decided to wait a bit.... First, their plan was to get back to the parlor basement. Tina expressed her interest in using some of the "secret jungle liquid" (Brought back from the research lab)! There was a dead body in the parlor basement... and she was going to try to revive the body....

Chapter 3

It was autumn. The time of year in the northeast region of the United States was Randy's favorite season. They drove back to Tina's parlor... and while chatting, they discovered that they both shared the love of this time of year. Tina showed excitement! She thought about what they were doing... it was interesting, she admitted that much to Randy. There were other important things, though. Tina decided that it might be better if they travelled to the east end of the "island" (the main island", where there were nice towns.... Small communities with hotels, motels, inns – located right on the beach, or near the beach. Spend a few days out there and make a few memories.... Walk along the beach, take in a movie, visit the aquarium, stroll along the beach in the evening (to see the sunset...

together). Randy couldn't, wouldn't disagree to that logic. Love is simple like that.

Things like that just happen…. it's a mystery (in some ways). Not much to think about, just something that feels correct! And it was correct. They agreed to do that…. First thing in the morning… after a good night's sleep… the long weekend would be nice. Tina was also savvy! She also had every intention to bring along the technical notes and findings, from the forest…. There were some trails out east that they wanted to explore…bike trails… along the trails were rare pine trees…. Some descriptions were discovered in the research note books! She needed to collect some samples to include in the "life solution" (as it was termed…. A solution of rare elements, herbs, forest bark, etc., all the things needed to bring death to life!). Randy planned to pick her up first thing in the morning, after he visited the gym! The routine training was changed, somewhat – to shock the anatomy, physiology…. That was a good thing. The human musculature had a very good way of adjusting to stress…. Every couple of months, Randy made some adjustments to the routine…. This routine focus included more incline during the jogging.... The weights were typically "heavy". Today, they were not so heavy. The muscles seemed confused (he thought... if muscles could "think", Randy smirked, then laughed... silly thoughts... but, the muscles were definitely "shocked"!). After the routine, he showered then made a b-line to the closest 7-11 coffee house. He picked up fresh French vanilla coffee, charged his system with the caffeine... then was in the front of Tina's parent's house within fifteen minutes... The sun had not risen, yet – it was close though.... There was something refreshing about that time of morning.... Many mornings were met like that, in Randy's mind.... The early morning was crisp – right before the official rise of the bright yellow sun! At that moment, the ground was sometimes wet with dew... the surroundings were absolutely quiet! It was just before the world woke...just before the birds chirped.... Just between darkness and the beginning of a glimpse of sunlight in the distance (Which, was not perceived as sunlight, no – just the shade of dark to grey, to light white in the sky...).

Tina left a note on the kitchen table, for her parents. It listed the name of the place they would be at for the long weekend (address, with telephone number). Next to the kitchen was a furnace room. She hurried into the room to grab a few bras off the line. Their house was modest. The kitchen had some basics... a refrigerator.... Cabinets.... And in the "furnace room", was a nice washing machine....no dryer. It helped save on the cost of electricity. She gently closed the front door and made her way to Randy's car – with bright eyes! (Looking-at the coffee!). They smiled at each other. It wasn't winter yet, the snow had not begun to fall in this region... football was just beginning... (she flirted with Randy, reminding him of the last snow fall, where she stood in the calm yard as snow landed all around them and on her cute eye lashes... which was followed with a tackle... Randy was showing her tackling drills when she aggressively tackled his solid 185-pound musculature – right into the snow! They laughed together and smiled as they sipped their coffee). Randy made his way to the ferry to get onto the main part of Long Island....

They got the motel room, right on the beach. Then strolled along the desolate beach.

The ocean was calm, but as far as the eye could see – a sight for "natural power". The ocean was amazing to look at... and as they walked the coast line, they looked out into the vastness of pretty ocean. It was a sight to see and to feel. They felt small, compared to such an awesome force of nature.... The sun was high in the sky – it was early afternoon... the brightness of the sun warmed them. Tina and Randy ordered some pizza... had it delivered to the room. It was perfect – fuel for the think tank. The pizza was filled with meat balls. The New York style pizza was delicious! And as they ate, Tina opened all the technical manual notes she had captured from the secret forest project.... The way she analyzed the data was impressive. It truly blew Rand's mind.... Technical literature and scientific data was like a "hobby" to her. She enjoyed reading through the stuff – it was simple to her. (The stuff was not simple). The findings... were... fascinating.

It was cell signaling! The research tapped into the human cell surface, and beyond.... The "life potion" from the forest incorporated natural chemical components that targeted the human cell surfaces. On the cell surface, there were immense "markers". Some, termed the markers... proteins. A recognition marker was like a key to a lock. Targeting the correct human cell marker started a "chain reaction". The reaction began with opening the lock at the cell surface. Once the "cell-signal" made its way through the lipid bilayer (the cell surface anatomy). Other reactions occurred.... Sort of like a trail of dominos getting knocked down. Only, there was one difference.... Some of the reactions created an "amplification" of the initial signal.... The final signal made its way away from the cell surface – through the plasma into the "nucleus". Inside the nucleus – the cell manufactured a "reactive component" – the information contained in the DNA, and to some degree, the RNA....

They stopped the technical discussion. Tina looked up and smiled with glowing eyes. The information was fascinating...they knew that. They also knew that there were more important things at this moment in time.... And it started with the soft kiss... she placed her wet lips on Randy's ear lobe.... They were only there a few days.... The time did not seem like only a few days, though. True happiness will have that effect on people... soul mates.... The motel was located steps from the open ocean! It was amazing. Tina left the bay doors open and the fresh ocean air made its way into the room. The simple plan for the extended weekend was to relax and do absolutely...nothing! Which was a great plan! As the sun was setting in the distance, Tina and Randy walked the shoreline and continued to discuss the research lab. It was odd to them. The front of the research seemed to be straight forward. Search for new plant species, herbs, roots, and the impact the "jungle" has on the surrounding ecosystem.... Some of the creatures living in the forest were also studied. However, behind the "research" there were other top secret studies.

What was troubling about the research was the "bodies" being donated to science. Cadavers from recent "accidents" were being brought into a chamber for tagging, bagging and transport to the jungle. However, the accidents were suspicious.... Many odd circumstances surrounded the deaths. And the mechanic was always in the equation. Car troubles, train accidents, failing brake accidents, pedestrian Accidents with cars that lost steering.... Just prior to the "accidents", the "mechanic" had serviced the vehicles! Tina observed some really nice beach rocks, pebbles and sea shells – as they walked and talked. Randy was happy. He would keep some of the specimens as a nice reminder of their long weekend. The shells would be placed on his desk or in his car – where he could see them....and smile as he would think back to that nice walk along the shore line... with Tina. The bike trails were a lot of fun! Tina collected a good source of tree bark, tree pine needles and various specimens.... To be used in the "life formula".

The parlor cellar was dark, and smelled of chemicals – the type used to embalm the dead. Randy followed Tina to the far corner of the dark, lifeless room... just behind her desk, was a bookshelf. It almost seemed "out of place", "out of sorts", for the room. And it was. Tina smirked, then winked. She did something to a series of the shelved books that initiated what appeared to be a secret passage. The passage was narrow, and they quickly entered – before it closed....

Behind the bookshelf, another place was found.... It was not of this realm.... It just couldn't have been of this realm... it seemed to be "different". For one thing, the lighting was so bright. Randy thought he was perhaps in a science fiction styled dream.... That only lasted a few seconds, though. It really just was the lighting in the narrow hallway! They were not in any kind of science fiction world.... It was odd, though.... The narrow hallway led to an operating room. The room had some cadavers in it. And was lined with refrigerators.... Tina was storing some specimens, not for fun. She was experimenting with the dead.... Trying to bring back the life! She pointed to a freezer... and in it were organs... the experiments started with cells, then grew to include organ regeneration. Finally, after much success she was able to start some of her research on whole human bodies!

First, she made it very clear to Randy... she needed his help with something. She asked him to open one of the freezers that was located away from the other freezers.... In it, he found a huge bag of weed. She wanted to smoke. They were occupied with the herbs for the rest of the night, and wound up falling asleep together – side by side, in the shape of a spoon. During the night, in the odd research room – with dead cadavers... Randy woke to the sound of a dragging foot... maybe not a foot... he thought it could be more than one foot... maybe, perhaps....it was feet! He looked next to him, at Tina... she was snoring... in a deep sleep... then he turned back toward the sound of something being dragged... he squinted his eyes... the lighting must have had been on a sensor, because it was almost completely dark in that room (he did not remember turning off any lights? Then again, it could be the weed talking...). He tried to fall back asleep... turning away from the darkness, snuggled into Tina... for a minute or so. Then, there it was again. Like a dragging sound... it startled him....The next morning Tina woke and showed Randy the "kitchenette" area. They brewed fresh coffee and had a light breakfast, together. The dragging sound came up in the conversation. Tina smiled and said to Randy, "you smoke too much...", then laughed. Randy smiled back, awkwardly. Perhaps she was correct... or not? He really wasn't sure. The sounds seemed pretty real to him. In any event, they agreed to one thing. They needed to return to the "forest" (or whatever that jungle research environment was) to get a closer look at what was happening there.

The town was located on an island, literally a "barrier island". The barrier (they say) has a protective nature to the main island... which was a short distance – viewed simply by looking across the ocean bay. This was good for the fishing industry. The island had access to the deep Atlantic-ocean, where plenty of deep-sea tuna were caught and sold for the bidding price. A good-sized tuna, caught in season that weighed approximately four hundred pounds...could bring in a 6,000 to 8,000 dollars prize! A living for many.... A good nutritional diet for others.... The mechanic had a machine shop, just near the local fishery docks.... The mechanic was a "jack of all trades". He was savvy with talk and was able to weasel his way into many homes.... Fixing decks, fixing lighting, replacing walls and floors.... The mechanics shop was local, and could fit two cars in the work station area. There was a lift in the back that was also used for boat work. The business was healthy, the clients were happy.... The island was plagued by a savvy murderer.

These days, the mechanic (David) was not doing most of the dirty work. At night he had hired help. Relationships with a population of people that were typically found in dark hole in the wall bars – that was his "circle". Those people had contacts in other dark communities.... The ties ran deep... connected to local news stations, local doctor offices, dentist practices, school systems... and the list went on and on... it included a group of what they called "women". They were not women, yet they had families, went to church, and were good at hiding behind the sacred goodness of what "a family should be". Other people, good people, did not suspect any of this "hidden workings within the island"; If they knew, they would have certainly left the island a long time ago... if they knew, they would realize that these "women" were not "women" they were part (if not a root cause) of the murders... if they knew, if the good community people truly knew... they would realize these "women" were "dogs". With intent to murder (sooner of years later).

There was a psychotic rationale to the murders (in their minds). Cash in social security benefits from an unsuspecting ex "man" (as these dogs called the gender, because they did not know what true love was... they could not, since they did not have souls or their souls were blackened with hate and evil). The rationale continued (in the minds). The "man" was simply not part of the evil community... the "man" challenged the "status quo". And when that happened! Boy, was there hell to pay! The first thing to do... was to bark at the local "mechanic". He would take care of it and ensure that a carefully planned "accident occurred", or a carefully planned exposure to some toxin occurred that resulted in an untimely sickness – terminal sickness....This "way of life" on the island had been in balance for at least fifty years (maybe longer). The history was not "documented". It was an unspoken, undocumented way of life. Except (of course) for the documentation needed to collect a 10,000 to 500,000 life insurance policy on their "man". In that case, there was always plenty of documentation! The mechanic was savvy... a smart murderer. He had ties to controversial groups – the black community, the homeless community, the suburban mom male hater community, the dog community, the jaded ex girl-friend community, the new anchor that hated men community, the males that supported jaded ex girl-friends/communities... and the list went on and on and on.... Yes, the mechanic was savvy... and the hooks were in all levels of the community....

During David's time in the "business", he learned to play a mean game of solitary card – (if he wasn't busy with his boots under an unsuspecting suburban mom's bed... when here man husband was out working for a living to support her manicure/pedicure routine). The researcher from University visited David – it was a late Friday night. Their meetings usually lasted ten to twenty minutes and were scheduled on a Friday night. David was quiet, yet his long dried yellow toe nails scratched the floor – easily, since the sandals revealed this one grotesque feature.... David asked the researcher if he needed more cadavers for his University work. He was also interested in his progress... Was the research closer to bringing the "dead back to life"?

The room, the mechanic's shop seemed basic – with modern tools. The lighting was decent. Although, as David's visitor entered this shop… things seemed to change, gradually – yet, with definitive levels of warped gloom. For one thing, the cool ocean air that made its way into the space became a more frigid, arctic like air – more stale, more heavy than light refreshing ocean breezes…. The visitor could see his frosty breath, as he talked…. David did not seem cold at all. In fact, he was more of a fire burning in the freezer like environment. That sat and talked. There were plans, plenty of local town plans. Getting dead bodies were not the issue. Spacing out the "so-called accidents" was the challenge. David did not really care, either way. Allergies…. That was a good one! David smiled, with a grotesque glee. Set the dinner or lunch with a known allergy! Add a sprinkle of the allergen to the victim's plate and abera cadabera… we have a cadaver! He continued to smile. The visitor looked awkwardly uncomfortable. Perhaps, it was just the frigid air… it was tough to breath. Terminal cells from a cancer patient….

Inject the cancer cells into another victim, during a routine procedure! There's another good one.... That sometimes took to much time for David.... He was more of the smoking gun type of animal.... Whatever the scenario was... it got the job done! The bodies made their way to the University research lab; aka, the jungle...and the experiments were carried out....It was going to be a long weekend, at the University – David ready with implementation of a series of high-level experiments. He asked David to join him, he would need his help. Not only with the bodies, transportation of the cadavers... but, also with the activation of wild animal corpses... as keen on death and misery David was... he showed a cautious optimism about the upcoming weekend....Tina and Randy left campus in Tina's car. It was going to be an interesting weekend, in the jungle. They had every intention of returning to the dark forest... with a plan. First, they stopped off at a much-needed coffee shop – the local 7-11. Coffee was good, fresh and there was a pretty good selection of flavors.... The French vanilla and peppermint mocha were added to the fresh liquid caffeine.... Tina was insisting on getting over to the parlor basement... she needed Randy to just spend one more night, with her there. He looked at her with fright! She giggled and asked what was wrong…. Randy said "don't you remember the dragging body sound in the middle of the night!" She laughed out loud and said "I thought you were joking!" He wasn't, but how could he resist the sparkle from her eye… how could he say no to this angel. And he thought… no matter what happened to them, from this point forward, he could never leave her… even the worst misunderstanding that might lead to him being in the doghouse…. He would probably (definitely) blame himself (even if it wasn't all his fault), sit at an apple bs bar, drink a lot of beer then… eventually catch a cab to her (their) home base and make up with a sensual kiss….

There was another dead body in the cellar. They walked along side it, while Tina reached for the cellar ceiling light. She managed to turn on the light… then directed Randy to the desk and the bookshelf area. They entered the passageway together and closed the door. There was plenty of space, and the lighting seemed to be sufficient. It's just that there was something strange about the surrounding. Perhaps it was the dead body in the next room? Randy couldn't place his finger on it.... They would spend the night there, and he hoped that he wouldn't wake to any dead bodies talking to him!Tina sat on the bed, which was located in the far end of the room.... She smiled... a nice smile that presented kindness to Randy. There was more to her smile, though. A mystique that always amazed Randy. She wanted to share a secret with him. Randy saw something different in her eyes when she said that. [Tina knew of some training Randy had been involved in.... government training.... She was fascinated, especially since she loved the conspiracy theories.... She did not know all the training... and she was right about the conspiracy theories... some of them... Randy thought, what if she knew? Really knew of the "capabilities" ...as some would call it.... And as he looked at her, he realized that she did know...].

Randy couldn't wait, so he just asked her.... "How do you know?". Her eyes widened and she smiled. Tina had been close to the parlor her whole life, and she had been involved in trying to bring the dead to life for a good two years! What she stumbled upon was a place Randy visited... not by choice, more by chance... more by "circumstance" and, as it was, that place was what some would call the place where we find out things about places and people... find out things that sometimes we should not know... should not find out... But, it seems, a higher more divine force has designed this place in such a way... designed this place as a "safety net", for good to fight evil. Tina was taken by surprise... she suspected that Randy was a walker... a soul that has crossed over... but, she needed to confirm it... And now they knew... Tina showed Randy her access point. She used the various chemicals from the forest, and captured energy from cadavers.... With the right application, she was able to show Randy how she crossed over... It wasn't like walking through a door.... It was more of a momentary thing that lasted a short time... while the chemicals traveled through her and Randy's system... they would cross over... as the chemicals/fluids became dilute in their systems.... They would return to the parlor....

They ingested the natural energy and within minutes found the "other side". In this place, the peace was not measurable....it would be to great to measure.... Peace and serenity.... The colors were sort of "grey and whites", perhaps, no color at all, yet artistic in a subtle way... the mountains were everywhere... as far as the eye could see.... Their bodies were there, together (perhaps it was just the energy with residual memory of their flesh... they were calm as they held each other's hands....it was almost like being in a landscape style painting... truly fascinating... [Randy was studying existential philosophy at the University, with Plato and Socrates....and all these great Greek dreamers... this was nothing like their writings... not even the poet, Dante from the 1300s... unless Randy didn't understand the writings... which, was possible... the grammar was similar, with differences in some meanings – centuries ago... it was a locked off place, not for entry...... maybe only a select few that could return to what we call "life", all the others that entered... well, that was a one-way ticket.... Although, Randy sensed a one-way ticket meant that if they did return, it would be a different life... with different energy... maybe? Maybe not? "The mystery of faith" (they say).

Central to the landscaped environment was a beautiful river... as big as the eye could see!

It was amazing and what a presence! It was bigger than the Mississippi river! Calm though, very calm – even though it moved with defiant prowess! Truly a wonder of the world (if this was a world?) … it was more like a place that was behind what we think of as "The world" … Randy never wanted to visit this place, never… it's energy, its "great responsibility" was immense. It was too powerful to contain in a single thought. Yet, there they were – hand in hand… looking around. There was more. People here, some people were waiting to move on to the next phase… next life… the eternal gates (as some say) … some here, were "suddenly" sent here due to evil actions… and this is one reason for Randy's visit… Tina's visit… she was someone who just happened to stumble through to it….And, as it were…. Randy was touched by a friend – in that touch, energy was transferred… and part of him remains attached to his friend… when he visits, the energy (in the form of his friend) – he always reminds Randy to let "Heather" know he want her to be happy… and that he loves her… (that is always clear, that is always an important part of the conversation) …. There are thoughts and glimpses of things that may or may not be known.... The workings of evil... for example, a sleepy guy (Randy thinks his name might be sleepy Jon or sleepy Jose or sleepy Josepi) ... His family is evil, with inner working of war in the middle east... a crook that has blood on his hands... he hides behind the church; he hides behind all that is good in this life, like a good marriage, like a good family. He is not good. In fact, he pits groups of people against each other – with social class wars, race wars and gender wars... He stood for nothing of value.... True values of America, the land of the brave – included a land where capitalism was envied by all nations... where the innovative spirit through hard work, education, service to country, and earned experience, mattered....

Perhaps, there was a link to Randy's friend's untimely death in the middle east... perhaps there was no link at all... either way, Randy never asked for this visit... it is a cross to carry... They spoke and listened to others that talked of David and the dark forest at the University... the murders and the evil experiments.... Tina smiled, she could hear all Randy's thoughts and she was amazed at this place, at Randy and others that visited them – near the calm river... Tina, being a good soulmate, reminded Randy that this is a good thing... hope for this life and the next... a reminder that life goes on and good does/will prevail... and soulmates journey together in this life and the next... Tina and Randy woke together, as the natural chemicals became dilute in their systems... they were thirsty... but, very relaxed... and happy. They rehydrated with lemonade, rested and enjoyed a nice night together – with no dragging body sounds. Tomorrow, they would visit the dark forest....

Chapter 4

The mechanic brought his shipment of dead human bodies to the University research lab. There was a loading dock, located directly behind the biology lecture hall. There, he met the researcher. They wheeled the cadavers into the service elevator. From there, the elevator reached the basement level. Down the long dark corridor, was entrance into the forest. The mechanic had seen it all, or so he thought. That is, until he was about twenty or so minutes in what seemed a dark – odd environment. There was no sunlight in there. There was no natural light in there. It was pitch black; with the exception of their flashlights – and good thing for that. Traveling along the dimly lit forest floor was challenging. There were "night lights" along the path; that gave a faint yellow-green glow.... At least, they could follow the path. The bodies were stacked in a high end "wheel barrel". The mechanic wheeled the bodies (three to five; it looked like….) over the path. Eventually, the mechanic and researcher (Chuck) reached the work station shed.

This place was a research facility. It was supposed to be a research- initiative; exploring the forest ecosystem. It was not that at all. It was an evil place. Where two (the mechanic and researcher) used resources to fuel the dead to life; the dead returned – but, were no where near the original state…. They were sort of in a zombie state… where some recognized "self" (who they once were) with a slap to the face or a punch to the gut… but, within five or so minutes… of returning to their original state, original person, they faded back into a zombie form… It wasn't like the movie "night of the living dead". These creatures were aggressive! High functioning with basic instincts. They were hunters, killers…. Similar to a high functioning ape – the mechanic thought out loud. These creatures were beginning to even scare the evil mechanic! The researcher laughed at the mechanic… although, it was kind of an awkward – uncomfortable laugh….

The researcher knew, things were getting out of hand…. He was debating to close down the experiments and run to Mexico. What he did not know, was… it had already been too late to do anything like that! The forest was dark. The forest was very much alive with basic instinct creatures. And…. They would not last the night…. The forest would certainly consume everything in it! Including the mechanic and the researcher!

Randy and Tina made their way to the University coffee shop. Of course! Coffee was needed. They chatted as Randy found a holiday blend of creamer (peppermint) to add to the coffee. It was sweet, and it was the best thing to add to coffee! They decided to leave the car in the coffee shop parking lot, which was only walking distance to the campus research building. As they strolled along the University paths, they admired the oak and pine trees. It really was a nice architecture…. Placing lecture halls and research buildings inside a natural forest. The sun beams made their way through the tree canopy and it was a sight to see – they talked and sipped coffee along the way….

Entering the research building, they felt a sense of "urgency". An unspoken feeling of distress. Randy called it his gift. Tina shared some of that…. She had that feeling too, when the environment turned evil…. The sense was not specific, but it was there – like a black cloud in a severe thunderstorm that was ready to drop an F5 tornado! The gift was similar to "common sense". Some would turn and run away. Some would stop and start to sweat. Randy and Tina were the type to explore! And that is exactly what they did… with caution. Randy opened his back pack, just prior to entering the basement research facility forest. He removed and opened a sharp knife. It was a good hunting tool. He brought two. One for Tina and one for him.

They entered the forest without the use of a flash light (they had lights, but did not want to be seen by any potential predators…). The path was dimly lit and they followed it, deep into the forest…. In the not to distance, Tina heard "growling" and what seemed to Randy as a pack of wolves circling their prey. In the near distance of this dark forest… Tina and Randy heard distinct sounds of snapping ground twigs, brush being moved violently from side to side under the heavy footprints of beasts... Whatever was out there was closing in on these two... and it would not be long.... Randy snapped his head to the side as a large grotesque looking animal (or was this thing human?) lunged at him! The beast sank its saliva drooling teeth into his neck. Tina screamed, then approached the beast – stabbing it with her knife... behind her a pack of animals jumped through the trees and brush... lunging in a very coordinated attack!

It was dark and quiet. Randy opened his eyes and woke. Next to him, Tina was sleeping silently – and he admired her cute little smirk/ smile as she dreamed. Her cute smirk was something special. He thought that there was a mystique about her.... And he loved that.... He wanted to, needed to learn more about her and would spend the rest of his life doing that. He smiled as his neck pulsed with pain. Then, he heard footsteps in the next room. The footsteps were followed with the dragging of what seemed to be a bag of bones or a bag of body parts.... Tina woke, turned on the light and smiled at Randy. Just before the light went on... Randy could swear that her eyes seemed to glow a fluorescent yellow... The lights revealed that they were in the basement of her family funeral parlor! She asked Randy what was wrong... He stopped hearing the sound in the next room... It was quiet again.... She repeated: "what is wrong with you?". He grabbed his neck and felt no wound, saw no blood.... He said "weren't we just being attacked in the research-forest?". She laughed at him... and said "I think you smoked too much of my freezer weed!" ... Randy smiled and laughed... awkwardly laughed as the room adjacent to them vibrated with another dragging sound....

The End.

The Iron

Written by Richard A. Boehler, Jr.

Chapter 1

The Earth was an amazing planet. A nice place to live, a wonderful place to carry on traditions, legacies, and raise a family. In the year 4020, the natural environment did not permit such luxuries... There were no choices for the human race to carry on in such a way. The Earth had changed to where the baseline survival of "life" was affected, with such dramatic circumstances. The world could have been ready.... The world, should have been ready. Unfortunately, the world was not ready for the "perfect storm". It was a combination of events that led to the total destruction of the "biosphere", that is the natural balance of life as we knew it. The global warming that melted the ice caps was one factor. The over population of the planet with poor resource planning was another factor. The building and use of nuclear weapons after another world war was yet another factor. And finally, the impact of a giant stone from outer space sealed the deal; sealed the fate for the world.

The world should have been ready for the worst, and hoped for the best. Luckily, there was a research project that was started (not completed) some years earlier – where colonization of an iron rich planet had been explored...

Mayport, Florida

There was no time, chaos had ensued and panic was evident. Tina and Randy made their way to the front entrance of the Naval base. The command (all commands) was in Defcon four mode. A heightened state of readiness, where security checks were held with robust precision and overhead helicopter patrols were more frequent than usual. It was necessary, to maintain order – in a world that would cease to exist in a short time. The affects of all the natural disasters were not clear to most experts. It was believed that the planet would certainly remain in a hibernation phase, for at least 100 years. Maybe longer. Similar to what might have happened during the historical ice ages (only with a multiplied factor of 100...). The human population, across the globe, would not survive. The human population – even with best efforts and known technological advancements – could not survive. Tina flashed her military badge and Randy did too, it was the first area of entrance into the base. The soldiers slid mirrors under their car and looked for anything suspicious.... A copy of the official sealed order was presented to the head soldier. He looked over the contact info, called into the area of the base to verify and then returned the document to Tina. Driving across base was peaceful (if that was possible during this chaotic time). Tina admired the base housing, located right on the shore. She was familiar with the base and the housing. Tina had trained over many years, with a destroyer squadron – and during some training cycles, she had bunked right in the shore front quarters. Each morning she would rise and jog the beach, then cut across the naval base...

[*It was a Saturday morning, and after showering she made her way to the galley for a late breakfast. It was her routine. Not just to rain "soldier fit", not just to stay up to par with physical readiness standards.... Not just for the peaceful view of military operations across the base – as she observed when she jogged.... It was for the time in the galley, food! The bases across the country competed with one another, to win the prize of being called the best galley! Tina did not know much about that competition, but she did know that it was clear that the Mayport Naval Base had*

one of the best galleys (across the country). The selection of food was simple, yet divine! Not common in a military setting. You were lucky to get a sandwich or a hot meal (in some cases). This base was different and the ships here were top of the top. Battle group ships with the prestigious label that was earned and evident. Ships with nuclear warhead capabilities. Ships with trained and readied crew to be called on at a "moments" notice... depending on global events.... Tina went along the galley line, selecting her food for this late breakfast.... Being careful to stay away from anything that might have a bluish color to it... (she had a bad experience with the effects of whatever they were putting in the food....). It was the investigative nature in her. After some time of investigation, she concluded that there was some kind of natural additive being placed in the food to reduce the senses of emotion. (She understood that sometimes it was critical to dull senses of emotion, but she did not like it. She stayed away from that type of food and kept a good healthy level of emotions).

Tina always selected the table near the open picture windows, while she ate at the galley. She had the best view of the soldiers hanging on rope ladders – outside rapidly flying military choppers! There was a guy she took a liking to, hanging from one of those choppers…. training on this Saturday morning… His name was Randy….

Randy stopped the car, near the MacDonald's. Yes, the biggest naval bases had MacDonald's located right in the center of military operations…. Sailors ate lot's of cheeseburgers…. Randy received an encrypted message from the command. The message advised to hang tight with meeting at the ship. The ship had been scheduled to set sail, immediately. There was no time to waste, and they all knew that. The stability of the planet would make things difficult. The ship was heading to some secret location off the coast of Florida…. From there, they would find out the next steps in the process.

For now, the plans had changed. Had been delayed for two days. So, the two changed direction – and found themselves in the lobby of the base BAQ. The quarters were nice, situated right on the Mayport Naval Base beach. Inside the room, Randy opened the sliding glass doors. The fresh ocean breeze blew into the room. The air was clean, salty and refreshing. The two had almost forgotten that the planet was in chaos. The beach water was at least 500 yards further out into the abyss. It was the oddest thing. Something was pulling the tide water's directly off the shoreline....

The most recent encrypted message from the command was read by Randy. Tina and Randy prepared for a few nights stay, in base quarters. After which, they would meet in the damage control central room – aboard a United States Battle Ship. Randy started unpacking when Tina demanded a night jog. She said: "get your shit, let's hit the beach for evening cardio. Randy laughed, but Tina only smirked at him. She continued, and said: "full gear, let's get this mother fucker started.... wear the heavy, steel tipped boots – and forty pounds of equipment". Tina smiled and giggled. You know the routine.... and they both did. The beach was always a nice place to walk along.... and admire the ocean, calm fresh breeze... perhaps a sunrise or sunset.... Cardio on the beach in full equipment... that was no fun....

actually, intense... after the forty minutes of cardio, Tina led Randy into the ocean.... for an early night's swim.... a romantic swim (yeah, treading water in sweat soaked equipment and steel tipped boots). After twenty to thirty minutes [what seemed like an hour, at least] they crawled out of the ocean, onto the shore. Laying on the sand, they both stripped to bare skin.... and just gasped for air, breathing and staring into the early evening sky, together. Tina reached for Randy's bare hand and held it.... They relaxed and enjoyed the natural surroundings... she was a feisty one, she was mysterious to Randy [he loved that about her].

They talked for a while, and expressed their fear of the planets end. The experts estimated that the "functioning ecosystem" would cease to function within six months to one year time frame. Randy and Tina were fascinated with ecosystems.... [even before the Earth was in trouble]. The balance of nature was a subject that included many different areas of science. Water, air, and soil were three very different and complex areas they studied.... The full moon lit the dark ocean below. Randy and Tina watched the ocean peacefully glisten all around them. Something was not right, though. Tina focused her attention on the horizon. There seemed to be turbulence in the water. Not ordinary turbulence that could have been caused by a Navy ship. Not ordinary turbulence that could have been mistaken by sea life splashing through the surface of water.... It was something else. Underneath each bare skinned body, the ground rumbled.... similar to an earth quake. The ocean followed the rumbling, pulling away from the shoreline. It was immediate! One second the crashing of calm sea was there.... the next minute, the ocean water pulled away leaving exposed sand and rocks as far as the eye could see!

Randy's phone notified them of a secret message. The travel into the deep sea, onboard the battleship was moved from the end of the week to tomorrow. The ships were located in a different part of the base. Typically, turbulence on the ocean (hurricanes) would prompt the ships to leave port.... ride out the storm. Staying tied up against the pier during a hurricane would result in structural damage to the ship.... sailing the rough seas was a better way to go in these circumstances....

Tina and Randy both knew that and decided to just relax their minds for the night. Tina smirked at Randy [he admired her smirk...] It was devilish (in a good way), the smirk was fascinating to him because it offered him a mystique. A mystery about Tina that he wanted, he needed to learn more about.... besides that, it was just adorable! Then Tina said "are you just going to stand there naked or are we going back to the barracks" (she giggled). Randy paused and laughed, looking at her fit body only for a moment.

[He was shy] Before he got too embarrassed to give her a kiss... they returned to the room, overlooking the distant ocean... The room doors were open, taking in the fresh ocean breeze (what was left of the ocean). Tina and Randy entered, then showered. Afterwards, they relaxed to soft music and a bottle of wine. Randy was always mesmerized by her sparkling brown eyes.... It literally melted his heart... and was complemented with gorgeous long wavy brown hair (sometimes with high-lights) [what a heavenly combination]. The wine helped set the mood. Not that it was needed.... Her eyes did that for Randy...

she was sensual and true.... A lover that connected her soul and heart – each time they were together. Something words could not accurately describe... a feeling.... The touch of an angel. They were soul-mates. She touched with amazing qualities... not only her soft hands... it was her lips, her tongue.... and much more... Randy and Tina shared a wonderful night together.

The ship was a first class battle-ship. With many different capabilities, including tomahawk missiles, laser guided missiles and a sophisticated defense system. Just to get to the place to enter the ship was a project. The stairs were enormous.... Tina and Randy started the long climb up the steps.... At the top, they each turned to the US flag (located at the far end of the ship) and saluted. Following the flag salute, they each saluted the officer on deck and asked permission to board the vessel. The officer saluted, checked their identifications and the presented paper orders.... The final check point was an electrical device that searched for illegal weapons... (they each presented their standard issued .45 caliber hand guns, prior to the final check point). They were met by one of Randy's buddies…. who asked them if they were hungry? Tina and Randy replied: "yes" and then followed their ship-mate into the first corridor. Inside was a maze of halls and stairs…. one could easily get lost in the ship…. however, after some years onboard US Navy ships… Randy and Tina were both pretty sure that they could navigate through the entire ship, blind folded! The three arrived in the galley, for breakfast!

There weren't many in the chow line. Randy knew it would be a skeleton crew for the trip out to sea. Many were on other orders, many were with family, many military folks understood that the end was near – so they took leave. A permanent leave. There were certain areas of the military that continued to operate, even until the end. This ship, would venture to an area within the Bermuda Triangle – where a top-secret facility housed a group of elite personnel. The chef asked what they would have for breakfast? Randy liked to order the eggs with vegetables, ham and cheese. It was a treat. He came from humble beginnings – not many people understand why something as simple as an egg dish would be appreciated. Most days (where he came from, where he was raised) were "pot-luck days". In other words, you ate what you could find. Not the healthiest way to live. In the military, there were three square meals each day (usually, unless there was some fierce exercise/operation). That was a good thing to look up to – for a kid from a small suburban town. Tina also appreciated the selection of food. Her beginnings were different, but humble – similar to Randy.

The three were seated at one of the galley tables. Eating their breakfast and initiating a discussion about the "mission". The ship was sailing…. and they would leave the galley to meet in a more formal briefing room. For now, they were enjoying the eggs and toast. The coffee was hot, brisk and strong! They needed the caffeine! Randy's friend Tony began to talk with detail. The ships full crew was two hundred. The current skeleton crew included approximately fifty. The planet's ecosystem was failing and the oddest things were occurring across the globe. Tony's anxiety levels were through the roof, with the simple fact that they were traveling to the Bermuda Triangle. Strange things happened there all the time, without a breakdown of the planet's ecosystem. Could you imagine what we might run into with the current planet's ecosystem? Randy said "calm the fuck down". Tina giggled – you two are goof balls! They all laughed. {they still had their sense of humor, that was a good thing! A gift during these dark times!}. {Tony was Tina's dad. They were close – a good daughter/dad relationship. Randy admired that about Tina – it spoke volumes to him. Tina was a brilliant lady – with a champions spirit. Words can't truly describe each element of "champion". But, if words could – she would define champion! It was evident in her eyes, in her cute sense of humor. Her words stopped Randy in his tracks…. Often (not always, but often). He would think…. to himself, did she just say what I think she just said? Then giggle…. It was the innovative spirit that pressed at the limits of knowledge, wisdom and understanding…. to create some controversy (some time, and other times, just to get people thinking). Randy thought of time together with colleagues – in a top-secret research projects. Real smart people.

And they were. But, there needs to be more than just smarts. It is the innovative spirit that burns deep in the soul that drives some great things…. Randy felt it, felt it his whole life…. It was a gift (and some times he just felt it was a curse….) that helped drive some great things in various fields of study. Randy saw that in Tina and thought that she would certainly teach him some things…. she was more, though. It was really the peace and serenity he observed in the sparkle of her eyes that first attracted him to her. Again, words don't do it justice. Some may search their whole lives for that peace and serenity in their partner … and may never find it! Randy was lucky…. It was from the heavens. She was an angel on Earth. His angel. There was more in her sparkle…. There was mystery. And that was another thing that attracted him to her. She seemed so mysterious to him (sometimes, not all the time). And he loved that. He wanted to learn more about her. She had charm, but was feisty at times… which was cute. Within that shine, that sparkle from her eyes he also saw kindness (with champion strength) and loyalty. And those are some words to describe Tina Rose. There was more, much more …. That words, would never be able to accurately describe. And that is where, the invisible connection, he knew that she was his soul mate, and he believed she felt that connection too. The connection that words won't describe correctly…. and that was okay with him because in her kiss, in her hugs, in her love – he was able to understand her, understand her and him – together}.

They finished breakfast, returned their trays to the conveyor belt and left the galley. Tony brought Tina and Randy to a part of the ship that housed small arms, weapons, ammo, etc. Randy thought it was cool that Tony's military specialty was "gunner". He was trained on each ship weapon, system that protected the ship from enemy fire and he just loved to talk about it – within his circle of friends/ family. That was good for Randy because he loved to listen to that kind of stuff! Randy's specialty was classified. For the outside, he was a subject matter expert in science, CPR, survival, medical readiness, administration, and instructor duties… He knew that Tina liked to watch him hanging from helicopters while she ate chow in the Mayport galley, though!

From the gunner's locker, Tony brought the group down many stairs – and through many hatches. The ship was a floating city. Along the way, they took note of the markings on corridor walls. It was okay, they had been on many ships – and could easily navigate through the passageways…. they arrived in the briefing room. Located in "Damage Control Central". Pretty much, within the heart of the ship…. There, they were greeted by a team of eight military commanders….

Chapter 2

- **The Mission.**
- **Top Side in the Moon Light on board the US Navy Battle Ship.**

Meeting like this, briefings like this were usually held prior to implementing a very strict set of military orders. Where those orders originated from was always a wonder to Randy.... Somewhere in the pentagon area, he supposed.... brought through various channels and eventually made the way into the briefing room. They all sat and listened. Times were different, times had changed. The world was in the last phase of implosion. Which meant chaos and uncertainty. The top scientists predicted about six months or maybe a year until the planet would not be able to sustain life. That was just the estimate though. As Tina and Randy listened, they winked at each other... a wink for intimacy, a wink for trust, a wink for the "soul to soul" connection. The wink was followed with a cute smirk from Tina.

The ship was headed into the Bermuda Triangle region. Within that area, they would dock with the research center. The building did not exist (at least for the purpose of real life). The team would leave the ship and board a shuttle. The shuttle would transport the team deep under water to the main research laboratory. The ship was sailing quickly, but still would need two days to get there.... the commander dismissed the team and they left for the barracks. Tina and Randy decided to continue with the PT (physical training). They changed into work out gear and started their jog around the ship. The top side of the ship was a good area to jog. They enjoyed the fresh ocean breeze as they jogged along the top surface of the Navy Ship. It was dark, pitch black out around the ship. High in the sky was a bright full moon. Their sneakers gripped onto the thick no skid floor, as they jogged. Forty-five minutes into the jog, they made their way into the barracks. The showers were designed to conserve water. One button to press, and hold to discharge the ships water supply. After water was dispensed, the button was released. They soaped up, then repeated the water discharge. The water was ice cold! Some-times, if they were lucky, the water turned warm. Tina brought Randy back to top side... they found a place to sit together and admire the surrounding ocean – lit by the light reflecting off the full moon. She kissed him and they embraced for what seemed like forever. [time seems to disappear during moments like that].

The ship was a floating city. A network of systems that enabled self-sufficiency. Heck, there was a few washing machines and dryers too! Within the PT area of the ship, topside, was a basic weight training room. A few bench presses, weights and squat racks. Good to keep the strength up! Between cardio jogs around the ship and weight training – the physical readiness was maintained. The entertainment room was simple, but good. A nice big screen television for movies. And some video game systems. The selection of literature wasn't that great, but there were some good books. Most military people brought their own selection of literature on board. Computers were there too, but depending on the mission... access to networks like the world wide web, were limited. There was always fishing! Depending on the sea and the location.... Throwing fishing lines over the side of the ship would result in the catch of some deep-sea fishes! The crew would bring the catch to the galley for cooking. One-year, Alaskan sea crab was caught and cooked for dinner! Very tasty!

As time passed, the air seemed different. The sky was changing and the earth seemed to have "tremors" [similar to earth quakes]. It wasn't good, the end was near. Tina and Randy talked about the Earth's history. The massive amounts of treasures collected through time. Including so many different areas of life: the arts, the music, the science, the literature, the movies, the wars fought, the freedoms won, the lives lost... the sacrifices... it was kind of sad. To think of human kind having to leave the planet. Sort of like a move from one place to the next. Anyone who knows anything about moving knows that it is no fun. It is a lot of work! To first go through all the junk collected over the years in one place, then move what was of some value to the other place (and discard the stuff you didn't want to transport in the move). Imagine sifting through all the collections of man- kind! Then transporting the important stuff to another planet. Who would decide what piece of art would be transported? or what books should be transported? Good thing, there was a team of people working on that some time ago, and many treasures were uploaded electronically then sent (in various redundant channels) to the next colony. The originals of some treasure (like art) were packaged carefully and sent via space capsules (unmanned space crafts with high tech transport instructions!).

Still, it just seemed kind of sad to have to move off planet. Tina and Randy were lucky. They had been part of this top-secret team for the past decade.... and now it was time to implement, it was time to take action, it was time for change! There were technical challenges, gaps (so to speak) with the transport plan. It was important to be able to bring the correct materials to the iron rich planet. A one-way ticket for colonization. There was no turning back, once planet Earth was in the rearview mirror. The materials needed to colonize the next planet were strong metals, chemicals to fuel various essential processes and equipment to filter/purify water, air and food supplies. And that led to the next challenge. The essential seeds for various food supply (vegetable, fruit, animals, trees, plants, herbs, bushes, etc.). That part of the program was completed and was presently being sustained in the atmosphere of the new iron rich planet. That ship circles the planet with a self-sustaining nuclear core, and a skeleton crew of about 100.

Being top-side on a Navy battle ship is quite a sight, quite a feel, that words can not accurately describe. It was sort of like those commercial cruise ships, with 100 times the power and two to four times the mass. Perhaps it was the battle gray blending in the ship to the ocean that added to the mystique. Perhaps it was the nuclear core that allowed for sustainability without extensive replenishment. Horizontal and vertical replenishment for necessary supplies were always a routine ongoing operation in the depths of the ocean. Which was achieved through ship to ship means and aircraft/helicopter to ship means. Power sourcing was no problem, with the nuclear core. Most ships (just about all ships) were equipped in this way.

Tina and Randy continued to sit top side in a private area of the ship. They were enjoying the fresh ocean breeze. The bright full moon, and even areas of star constellations were very clear in the night sky (with the full moon). It was amazing. There was no light pollution in the deep ocean. No city lights, no shopping center lights. No airport lights. The night sky was there with more stars than they had ever seen before. The only source of light in the sky came from the very bright full moon. Which was also a sight to see, in the deep ocean!

They looked out into the dark sky where constellations painted an elegant scene. They Had been closing in on the Bermuda triangle region, when they noticed two things... first, there was more than the sound of ocean and fresh breeze in the air. Tina thought she heard a howling, in the distance. Randy heard it to. It was more of a growling sound to him. A few minutes passed, when they heard a dark low howling.... again. Tina and Randy were sitting close to one another. After the howl, they remained seated – topside – closer, hugging. Tina shivered. The second oddity was a flash of light, in the distant night sky. It was possible that the light was somehow being generated from the Bermuda research facility. But, they had not gotten too close to it... not yet, anyway. It was a good day. They knew what they needed to prepare for and they would continue their physical training. After leaving the flight deck, they ventured back inside to the galley. Although the galley was only open for three square meals, each day, there was always fresh brewed coffee! If caffeine was not what the crew was looking for, there was also a selection of "bug juice". So, they called it. Randy wasn't sure why they called it bug juice. There were usually one or two concoctions of each juice with funky colors. A bright red or a dark purple were commonly seen in the galley. It was sweet so Randy liked it. The bug juice quenched the desire for sugar... or what was called a sweet tooth! While seated in the galley, a group of military people rushed into the room, and abruptly closed each room hatch. They were locked in the galley! In the adjacent corridor a loud howl was heard. It was followed quickly by a grunt and door scratching. The door was metal and whatever was scratching against it must have been something fierce! The scratches were constant – and lasted only about five minutes... then disappeared....

The ship was entering a storm. The ocean was noticeably rough, as the ship listed from side to side. While navigating through the storm, the crew made their way to the bridge. There was a clear view of the stormy ocean from this area. It is amazing how fierce nature can be, at times. On land, tornados and hurricanes were good examples. In the sea, there was nowhere to go. The ocean was more fierce-then one might imagine. A rough day at the beach, where large waves crashed onto the shore line would not compare. Deep in the ocean, during a hurricane or a really bad storm – the water literally would engulf a large steel ship. The ship they were on was a monster. It was built that way. The steel beams, the technology was state of the art. The size of the ship could be compared to a cruise ship. Looking at cruise ships for vacations... the people boarding might be amazed at the immense space! These commercial cruise liners were something to see. However, when compared to the Navy ship Tina and Randy were on... It could have an estimated size differential of about three to four times the size of the commercial boat. The captain made his way aggressively through the storm waters. There really was no other way to do it. Any less aggressiveness would certainly result in the ship being at the bottom of the ocean. Some would call that place: "Davy Jones locker". It was basically science and art. Cruising through storm waters required an understanding of navigation procedures... with a side of art. The storm passed, or maybe the ship made its way through it completely.... weather patterns seemed strange.... the world was ending and there was much uncertainty. When events lead to an ending... there is one certainty....

Randy and Tina spoke about that certainty for hours, as the ship quietly made its way through the night.... The one certainty was "chaos". God only knew what chaos would be waiting for the skeleton crew, as they approached the secret research facility. As the great ship approached the research facility, they were in a state of calm. The storm was gone and they were ready to embark on another adventure. Transport from this earth to the "iron planet". It would be a fascinating journey. Not like the movies, though. Where cliches of frozen body storage was needed to sustain and survive the long trip. It just was not like that. Technology found a way. An out of the box thinking sort of way. They achieved space travel in a more efficient and effective manner! The crew was getting ready to dock with the research station. Most of the skeleton crew was in another area of the ship, throwing lines over the ships side.... and getting ready to secure the ship to the dock. Randy, Tina, and a few others stayed top side. This small group continued to monitor the weather and ship instruments....

The world was not a pleasant place. Was it ever really a pleasant place? Randy knew that. Some knew that. Leaving the comfort of "home" (quote unquote) to train in cold steel environments (so to speak....) made that abundantly clear to them. They were saddened by the recent events that led to the near end of the planet. What they did not give much thought to .... was counter intelligence. The United States was not the only nation ready to implement the contingency plans – to assure survival. There were other nations. In the distance, a Russian battle ship was observed from top side. The Russian vessel was not friendly. Within seconds, fifty caliber shells made their way to the ship Tina, Randy and crew were on! The small skeleton crew was targeted by some of the shots. From the interior bridge, Randy observed the skeleton crew be vanished. Along with the ship's water tight integrity! The ship lost water tight integrity and would be at the bottom of the ocean soon. Just prior to making their way to the life boat – The satellite guided missile defense system ejected a lethal blow to the Russian ship. Within mere twenty or so minutes – both ships were at the bottom of the ocean. The research facility was blown to bits and a four-person crew was on board a life boat – floating in the middle of the Bermuda triangle!

Tina and Randy were seated close to one another. Very close, interlocked were their fingers.... The other two that remained were silent – looking out into the distant sea... searching for any signs of life, any signs of a military presence. Perhaps another ship, perhaps a submarine that is usually accompanying a battle ship, within a group. Nothing. There was just the sound of ocean and wind. It was emotional to the four. A devastating blow to the ship, to the research facility. Not rationale. Just crazy. How to prepare for such chaos? What other measures can a vessel take to guard against a rogue Russian destroyer ship? They talked about these questions for some time, as the life boat floated in the open ocean. The group thought that maybe, just maybe the research facility was still intact. However, that theory was quickly crushed when they witnessed an emergency beacon pop up through the ocean surface. The beacon signaled imminent danger and was followed with chunks of facility parts floating to the surface. All was lost and there would not be much time until the very end of the planet. Randy laughed.... His way of trying to find a silver lining. Tina's father was not amused. Tina hugged Randy. Randy extended a firm handshake to her father – with a grin.

The grin was returned. We are taught many things in survival training. That is good. We might have a chance…. Randy spoke calmly. His humor subsided to a level of seriousness. To a level of humbleness. At the University, population dynamics was studied… at nauseating depth. I had a friend, Chris. He was taking the class for shits and giggles. Randy said that the competition was fierce at the University. Not just against global minds (from Russian, China, India, Japan, etc.) but also just against yourself.

In order to survive the curriculum, one needed to come up with broad spectrum strategies (more than one strategy, that could offer a synergistic result!). Randy continued to speak. The others (including Randy) were in shock, but reached a level of calmness. So, they listened…. this guy Chris was a wiz. Randy met so many great, smart people. Some that even had common sense! Others that could not find their passion, would not take a pragmatic path…. so, they drifted…. there were two he remembered that stood out in his mind.

Two University students that truly blew his mind. These two were more than just smart and more than just practical. They were super wizzes! Like something out of a comic book! His friend Anya was one of them. Ironically, she was from Russia. This guy Chris studied with Randy in a class that covered species population dynamics. In English, what the class covered was use of extinction models (computer models) to predict the population dynamics when/if a catastrophic event occurred... take some examples... a population of animals living in a jungle will thrive.... happily, the species will grow with a supply of food, shelter, etc. Now, introduce a catastrophic event! A forest fire that wipes out the entire species, except maybe for a few? With that scenario, the computer model is used to predict survival of the species.... it gets more complex. Introduce consideration for survival mechanisms that develop, due to the catastrophic event! Evolution! Some think that evolution takes time.... years.... hundreds to thousands of years! And that is true. But, not with all scenarios.... you see, there are catastrophic events that propel, that drive a shift in genetic mechanisms...

propel it instantly! Maybe a mutation occurs in the new species (the ones that survived) to have a greater tolerance for heat? Or maybe something else... it is a fascinating area....They looked wide eyed at Randy. He smiled and said "here is the silver lining". We survived.... Now let us find a way to thrive! The crew (all four of them) held hands and smiled.... They did not know how they were going to survive. Or what they were going to do.... but, they knew, at that moment in time.... they would find a way!

Chapter 3

All was not lost. They were alive and there were some lyophilized rations to eat on the boat. The group felt calmer, and more aware of the situation as the hours passed. There were no signs of enemy vessels. It was quiet in the Atlantic-ocean. The boat they were on was a military small boat.... not too sophisticated, compared to a Navy Ship. But, it did have some basic equipment on board that would help them get to their destination. An onboard navigation system was helpful. The fuel was good. The engines were running full speed ahead. They were in route to the northeast Florida Navy Base (Mayport). The trip would not take too much time. They decided, though, to proceed cautiously. In military terms, one strategy is to darken the ship. They moved at night – and kept talk to a whisper. The lighting for the interior parts of the boat was in a darkened mode. To the distant observer – they would just see the horizon blend in with the battle gray exterior of the boat. The two senior people navigated the boat, while Tina and Randy went inside to rest.

Can you believe there is a portable coffee maker on this boat? Randy smiled as he prepared the coffee. Tina laughed and said: "only you would make a pot of coffee in a time like this….". She was cute. Everything about her. It was her mystique that Randy loved the most about her. The sparkle in her eyes was what initially attracted him to her. There was so much more, though. The way she said things, the controversial topics (sometimes) that she presented…. He often found himself thinking… (did Tina just say what I think she just said…. it would make him smile, instantly! It blew his mind…. That was brilliance, that was a splash of champion…. the things that people don't always take the time to notice…. Randy noticed…. it was another quality that attracted him to her….) not that there weren't many other things he loved. She knew just where and how to kiss him. With just the right amount of zest. He returned her kisses. They were going to make it.... someway... getting to the Navy base was a good start. There were resources there. People they could talk to. Randy was thinking that he would get in touch with a command that specialized in covert activities. Their recent missions were somewhere in the north eastern mountains, the Adirondacks. Up there, way up north – just before the Canadian border – there was another research facility. Randy suspected that if they could find their way to that facility, they would have a chance to get a one-way ticket off the planet....They estimated the trip to be close to two days of travel. Randy and Tina rested on a sleeping space. What else could they do? They needed to conserve some of their energy for the upcoming days. They really were not sure what to expect, when they arrived on the Mayport Naval base. The scientists estimated the "end" within six months. That was four months or maybe five months ago... chaos was already being observed. When they got to the military base, it would not be a surprise if all surroundings were destroyed by looting.... The interior base should have remained organized. Who really knew what to expect?

It was the end, and even military personnel might leave to be with family....The crew pressed on diligently. Randy and Tina rested for some time. Then woke to the sound of crashing waves against the hull of the boat. Sometimes the sea was not so pleasant. The weather patterns were changing with the planets end, and that was starting to concern them. Topside, the four gathered.... The boat made its way through the storm and within a short-time they were close to shore. As they approached the shoreline, they immediately noticed that the base seemed desolate – abandoned. It was an odd thing to witness. The navy base housed battle ships and large air craft carriers. Any base has round the clock security.... round the clock fly overs with various military aircraft... operating with staggered frequencies.... and since the end was near – Defcon at the highest level should have been active. There were no active aircraft in skies. Most of the ships were missing.... no sign of personnel on base was apparent, as they left the small military boat.... The four man/with lady team arrived at the BAQ building. A place where some visitors slept. Sort of the military equivalent to a Hilton Hotel.... minus any real luxuries.... Randy and Tina just needed clean quarters, and a coffee pot! They were happy. The plan was to get a good night's sleep, find some supplies for their upcoming trip.... and locate a good military hum vee vehicle.... it was going to be a road trip, from Mayport Florida – up to the Adirondack mountains.... They needed to find the northeast research facility, if they were going to have any luck in getting off this planet – before it perished...

It was early evening, and the sun was setting in the western horizon. The colors were magnificent – spreading purples, pinks and oranges through the sky. The water was calm and the sea breeze was refreshing. If we didn't know better, it could be assumed that the world was perfectly okay. But, we knew. There were only months left, maybe less before the end would ensue. So, for now – Randy and Tina tried to relax. They enjoyed a walk along the Mayport Navy base shoreline. After leaving the beach, Tina and Randy decided to explore the base. They walked along paths that led to a galley. This was a headquarter galley, where different branches, various units ate meals throughout the week. Units from

Navy, Airforce, Coastguard, Marine Corp and elite service company teams: Navy Seals, and others.... In the distance, they spotted the large galley building. As they walked, it was odd to not see activity. There were no military vehicles driving the streets.... There were no personnel marching on the roads.... There were no groups of people jogging, running. In the sky, there was no military aircraft (no helicopters, airplanes)Tina and Randy always enjoyed the morning jogs around base. As the sun was rising in the eastern sky, and the world seemed to spring to life – they jogged together. Not too fast a pace, but with a good distance. They clocked most jogs between two and six miles. Depending on the condition of their muscles (from previous exercising). These days were different though.... These days, the world did not seem to spring to life. There was a calm in the air. Like, the wild life had left – the way they do when winter is approaching in the northeast. Like, birds flew somewhere for shelter. The insects were scarce too. There were no military personnel, as far as they could see....

In the chow hall, as some called it – there were showcases for deserts. Randy was experienced with that! He had a sweet tooth and loved the selection of sweets in the refrigerated show case. It was a tall refrigerator with glass walls. So, as the interior shelving turned in a counter clockwise fashion – the dessert could be viewed. When they spotted a dessert or two they liked – they would open the glass door. The interior shelving stopped turning as they pulled out the dessert to place them on a nearby plastic tray....At least the desserts were fresh. Randy selected lemon pie, while tina grabbed vanilla pudding. The refrigerator temperature was near ice cold – so the dessert was cool to the taste! They enjoyed the desserts as they sat near a window table.... Looking outside at the quiet world. They really were not sure of the big plan, at this point in time. There had been some discussion, but no real decisions that were definitive.... collect some canned food items and non-perished food for the trip? Tina's dad was busy looking for a military transport vehicle. Something with four-wheel drive capability. He found a nice camouflaged Humvee – it seemed like a tank! It would guzzle some gas. But that was okay, it ran on diesel and they would fill up some extra fuel cans (reserve fuel for the trip up north)The group decided to take two humvees into the Adirondack mountains. The "supply vehicle" would be packed with food and survival items (antibiotics, medicine, etc). Randy and Tina volunteered to drive that vehicle. Randy's dad and his friend were driving the other vehicle. Their Humvee would carry the extra supply of fuel. It was a good two day drive up north. They planned to avoid major cities... some which had been targeted by the nuclear arsenal.

This sort of trip would not be all driving. They went and headed north... following Tina's dad: Randy smiled at Tina and repeated... this sort of trip is not all driving.... He added some detail to his general statement. The road trip is about two to three days.... There will be lots to talk about as we drive..... lots to talk about. Fun stuff. Stories, conspiracies, ghost stories, life lessons, awkward moments. It turned out to be nice. They bonded together. When they were not listening to music in the car, and when one was not napping... they were talking and listening to each other. Amazingly, the trip seemed to go by so fast that before they knew it, they were approaching the Catskill mountain region. Just about four hours south of the Adirondack mountains! They pulled into a rest area to find some snacks. The rest station had fuel, bathrooms and vending machines. They were able to get more fuel for the vehicles, wash up and stock up on sugar filled snacks!

There was something different with this region. It was always "untouched". Randy often called it "God's country". It just felt that way. He supposed that one could debate that every area on the planet was "God's country". But, there was something special about the northern most region, the north east region. Maybe it was the altitude, or perhaps it simply was the air quality. The air was fresh, cool and "new". The breeze came from Canada, which wasn't too far from where they were headed. The trees were a sight. Pretty pine trees and oaks as far as the eye could see – rolling over mountains-immense forests. And deep in one of the mountain forests was the facility they would need to find.

After washing up in the rest area, eating and talking.... They decided to rest, take a power nap. Tina and Randy had plenty of space in the Humvee. They entered.... and the rest was needed. They smiled at each other. Soulmates have a way of knowing what thoughts are, without words. She was perfect, Randy thought... of course, what angel isn't "perfect". All her features... from her bright eyes, and shiny long brunette hair – to her soft lips, cute ears ... [and parts Randy knew he shouldn't be thinking about.... But, just couldn't help it....]Her features drew him in... not just her skin and perfect breasts... her light that completely absorbed his inner soul, heart and mind... sort of like a flash of light that never went away.... an intense light that was bright, intense.... not too intense – just enough to invite him into her love and keep him there.... forever.... and that (if a definition existed) was a good definition for an "angel babe". He rested his head near her heart. Randy felt her heart beat.... it was fascinating to him because his heart was in sync with her heart. He could feel the heart beating together. Just below his head he could see the necklace she often wore. It was pretty, a shiny golden cross. A piece of heaven. They slept peacefully for the next five hours...(more than a nap, a state of peace and serenity).

When they woke, they were surprised to being stared down by the other two team members! It startled them! Tina's dad had a smirk on his face.... a happy smirk (which was good – Randy hoped...) They needed to get to the research facility because the planet was beginning to change... noticeably change.... They could feel the shift in weather patterns... it was odd.... way up in the mountains, the cool weather became cooler and some of their vehicle gadgets were showing changes in the planet's temperature, just south of the Adirondacks – and beyond. From New York down to South America... So, they headed out quickly and arrived at the mountain research facility within two hours travel....

The facility seemed abandoned. No guards at the secret gate (which blended into the landscape). Randy opened the security booth, found the release lever for the front gate. They drove about a mile into the campus and found the main building. Something was not right. There is no way anyone could just enter a government research facility like this.... They would be greeted by military personnel, guns, dogs, aircraft.... especially in a "top secret" facility. There was just silence... Tina's father knew all the protocols and he had his ways, his techniques to get into the facility.... They were walking down a stairwell within twenty minutes! The stairs led them to another dark corridor... which brought them to a manual elevator. The elevator was a connection to another floor in the facility, which led to a generator powered elevator that literally must have brought them twenty miles+ deep underground. Deep in the bunkered research facility they met a group of scientists.... They didn't seem surprised, which meant that eyes were on Tina and her team from the beginning.... as they entered the campus grounds...Tina's dad was greeted – they all knew him, they saluted. The briefing started immediately, it was urgent. Apparently, there had been more going on with the world than anyone really knew. Rogue Russian military were sabotaging the efforts to leave the planet. Some rogue military made their way to the "iron planet", where they had bad intentions. The colonization at the iron planet was being compromised and most people knew nothing about it.... there was something else, though. Something that was not of this world. A dark entity was observed out there... and the scientists were not sure it was safe to leave "Earth" to arrive at "the Iron Planet".

Chapter 4

The situation was not a good scenario.... they thought that things could have been better. There were what some would call "the cards they had been dealt". It was up to the crew to figure a way to get off the planet. The research facility was built right into the Adirondack mountain. It was designed to be a secret laboratory, deep in the mountain base. The grounds were surrounded and hidden by pine trees, brush, rocks and more rocks.... Deep inside the research lab was a wardroom. A place where they met to discuss the next steps. The group of scientists there were not just your ordinary science type personnel. They had been trained in military combat, small arms and various weaponry. Biological and radiological defense measures. A good group to be around, especially since they were about to head to another place.... in space, where evil lurked…. the briefing was intense. There were videos played that clearly showed the Russian efforts to sabotage the entire space program. There was more. An evil entity…. a "dark leader" that was viewed in one of the rare videos. His group left to sabotage the "iron planet" colonization….

As often is the case, "what can go wrong, will in fact… go wrong…. multiplied one hundred-fold". The basic "murphy's law"! And they all knew that, they were all trained for that, of course…. they expected that…… It was just unfortunate that things could not have gone smoother. Instead of the peaceful colonization of the iron planet, a group of rogue Russian militia murdered most…. At least, that is what the group in this mountain research facility gathered with all the video footage. What really had happened was waiting for them on another planet. When they would arrive, they expected to be attacked, aggressively…. unless, they could find a way to travel discreetly…

They had time (someone said, as others giggled uncomfortably….) -truth was that they were not sure how long planet Earth had? Best guess was approximately one month. Not one person in the research facility could really estimate the end, though. There was one certainty... and that was: "the end was coming, and it would be sudden!". The group decided to rest and enjoy some "free time" for the next week. After one week, they would rendezvous back to the research facility wardroom... to discuss the scientific details of travel to the iron planet. But, for now.... They would all "surf". Randy and Tina talked about visiting his parent's summer home, just north of the lake George region. And that is exactly what they did. Not a second more had passed, after the briefing.... They said their good byes .... The Humvee was a perfect vehicle for the trip around and through the mountains! It was a road trip. Tina's dad stayed back with a few others to iron out some of the travel plan details.... Tina and Randy gave their hugs.... one week would pass by to fast.... so, they didn't want to waste one minute of the time.... There is something special driving along the mountain round in the Adirondack region. Perhaps it is the fresh mountain air. Perhaps it is just the pretty scenery.... Tina and Randy couldn't put their fingers on it, but it was something.... a unique feeling people got when they appreciated nature in this region. It was mid-day and in the distance they could see the rolling mountains. The mountains were covered with green pine trees. And as they looked, shadows from the nearby sun could be seen. They thought, if a person stood on top of the mountain (the very tip...) they might just be able to reach out and touch a nearby cloud! The clouds travelled so close to the ground. Or was it, that the ground was closer to the clouds! (that was probably it... they were literally in a mountain!)... A perfect place for an aspiring artist that enjoyed painting landscape scenes (Tina thought)....

The world was ending, but Tina and Randy were going to enjoy as much of this place as they possibly could. The main road they drove on was called the "north way". Truckers drove along this road... straight up to the Canadian boarder and back. It was a big truck delivery route for various supplies... including lumber. As Tina drove the Humvee further north, they noticed that the exits (distance between towns) grew. Eventually, they arrived at the correct exit and turned into a gas station. The station was abandoned, but they were able to transfer some additional diesel fuel into the reservoir. It was a modest house (once a trailer that had some mileage on it). The previous owner parked it, raised it, then built a strong cement foundation for it. The home was "stationary". Around the home, a fence was built, a front and back deck and a roof. It was a modest place, but it was nice. Tina brought her things inside and Randy followed. She showered first, then they cooked a basic meal together. There was a living room with two couches, and a picture window. Natural light from outside the home shined in. The kitchen was right next to the living room and it had a stove, refrigerator.... cabinets and a small space where a round kitchen table was placed with four chairs. Just past the kitchen was a hall that led to one bedroom (with bunk beds) and the last room (the master bedroom). They went for a walk along the neighborhood paths. It was empty. Everyone seemed to have disappeared. Tina was thinking that this was sort of strange. Thinking about their travel from the Florida state line, up the east coast... and now into the northern most part of the United States... the Adirondack-mountain region. She wondered where everyone went? Many people left the planet to colonize the iron planet. But, not everyone? Souls were missing.

They started a camp fire, after returning from the walk. It was getting dark. The cool mountain breeze turned even cooler. The fire warmed the area. Tina and Randy pulled two chairs close to the campfire and relaxed. She started in with her "conspiracy theories". Randy loved it. He honestly could just listen to her talk about ghosts, government conspiracies, lizard evolution, alien encounters... for an eternity! It was cute. When he thought about it.... the ideas were not all that too far from things that may or may not be completely true.... her stories made him think... her stories calmed him.... it was like peace and serenity.... A light from her that calmed his soul.... He loved that the most... that connection in many things they did together....The next morning, they woke with a cool and fresh mountain breeze – as it passed through the bedroom window... there were birds singing in the pine trees, just outside. It was a nice way to wake in the morning. Being with bright souls, good hearts and a surrounding with the crisp sounds of nature. In the kitchen, fresh brewed coffee created a morning scent of energy…. Randy started cooking some breakfast on the stove, when the door was abruptly opened. It was Tina's father! He quickly closed the door, sat at the kitchen table and asked for a cup of coffee. Politely, but they knew something was not right. The morning breakfast in this serene mountain environment became a "military briefing" for Randy, as Tina joined them at the kitchen round table. They listened. They thought that her father was staying behind to work on the travel plans…. to ensure that travel to the iron planet would be "perfect". That may have been a goal. But it was not the only thing on his mind. The group of scientists in the research facility did not seem like the same group he had remembered…. and he was correct. Some were Russian. Some were German. And none of these soldiers were familiar to him. So, he explored and discovered that it was the rogue Russian military! The same group that had destroyed the research facility in the Bermuda triangle! It got worse. They stopped to add fresh, hot coffee to their mugs….

There was no research project. It was just what some call "PR" (public relations). The goal was to ensure that panic was not promoted …. as the world came to an end. The goal was to present to the "people" that there was "hope". Hope for travel to another planet, "the iron planet". Where colonization would take place and where they could "survive", "thrive", and "grow" together – as a species. As humans. However, these people were not human. They were something else. Something… not of this world. And the "whatever they were", were camouflaged into the Russian military! Randy leaned back in his chair, sipped fresh hot coffee and smiled. Not that it was happiness…."well, this certainly changes things…!" They laughed (not to make light of the situation…. they just understood that it was now time to regroup, and improvise the PLAN)The group went for a walk around the neighborhood. [not that it had any people in it…. not that there were many homes, anyway. They were one hour north of a tourist region, called "lake George". And in the northern Adirondack mountains, there were certainly two things that could always be found…. Caves and wolves. About twenty minutes into the walk, they found the path to a nearby cave. It was hidden from the small neighborhood. Not, that the cave was much of a secret (it wasn't). The natural caves of this region are where they were created (from ancient times) …. however, Randy smiled at Tina. Tina knew of a conspiracy theory for this cave. Or was it more than a theory? The cave held something very special… deep in a network of caverns…

Sometimes in this life, things do not just happen by chance. People may recognize that "coincidences" do occur and they are probably correct with these presumptions. Other times, people and places come together for something much greater than a first glance would lead on to believe…. The right people, the right energy, the right circumstances…. The group didn't completely understand all of it… but, they did feel that the direction they were headed toward was "destined". Sort of a manifest destiny. There was no way to stop the impact on the planet. There was no way to stop the rogue Russian military and the evil that existed. There was, however, a trail that brought them deep into the mountain. And in that mountain was a facility with just the right tools. Just the right experimental knowledge. Just the right information to maybe…. just maybe…. help them survive. They met others, they talked, they shared knowledge. They ventured deep into the mountain and found interesting things. There were times when they left the caves and walked many paths in the sun light. The mountain breeze with surrounding scenery was stunning to this group. Time seemed to have stopped in this area. Time almost did not exist, with the exception of memories. The memories kept the group "grounded" (a figure of speech). And one night, a group decided to head back to Randy's parent's house. They enjoyed a camp fire, beer, liquor and ghost stories. When it final hit them. The fact that from what they gathered, together.... and after much discussion, philosophy, thoughts, laughs, serious talks... the fact that what they gathered was.... they never really made it out of the Bermuda Triangle!

Their physical bodies, that is. Their energy, on the other hand... well, their energy was there, up in the Adirondacks...

The End

The Pilot's Story

∞

Richard A. Boehler, Jr.
12-04-2021

Ecology class; the university research site.

Chapter 1

It was the 1980s when Michael experienced the first trigger point. A memory of something that could have happened, might have happened.... did happen. The thing was, it couldn't have happened in the 80s. Michael was just a kid, flying a kite. It was a brisk autumn day – a Saturday morning. The sky was a crisp, deep blue with puffy white clouds. A cool breeze brought the scent of local farm produce into the neighborhood.

Michael lived in the development, which was located less than one football field length from the patch of corn stalks, growing tall. His friends liked to fly kites. He didn't, not so much. He did enjoy nature, being out in the fresh air – and certainly admired the sky. As the kite sailed, as it caught gusts of wind – it elevated high above any tall tree canopy..... it was okay, they were positioned in the perfect area for "kite flying". It took some time for the kite to be raised into the blue sky. But, it was finally there – and it was absolutely beautiful to observe! Michaels buddy, Randy had been his friend for quite some time…. They had been through a lot together – in their very long lives of 12 years! Some great memories included (but were not limited) the building of the most sophisticated street ramps out of what they could find. Pieces of plywood, rocks, crates…. Then, the design came. An incredible space was typically set between two ramps. One ramp to incline the bicycle into the air and one ramp to catch the bicycle after spending time flying though the spaced air! Of course, the second ramp never turned out that well. It was the spacing! To much space between ramps was a terrible design. Or, maybe not so bad. The adrenaline rush of being propelled into the air was worth the thrill! …. that is, until the bike crashed violently into the second ramp (just short of landing smoothly). After the crash, the kid would fly off the bike – scraping skin, smashing bones along the concrete street….Randy's friend ran into the house to use the bathroom. He had asked for help with his kite, before he took off... Michael passed the line to Randy... who reluctantly grabbed it. The kite was so high into the sky, it was barely recognizable. Michael must have let a good seventy to eighty percent of the line out before leaving... and at that age, what experience does a kid have with flying a kite? Yet, as Randy observed the crisp blue sky – with a kite somewhere up in a very high altitude.... It occurred to him. Serendipity? De ja vous? He had been there before. That altitude, that crisp blue sky, that sheering cross-wind. Although, it was a different time – a different place. And, it was not a kite! What was high into the crisp blue sky was a plane! A military style fighter plane (good for its time), that flew dog style missions for strategic wins during a war... a war he was not that familiar with (at least, not yet) ... something dreadful had happened during that "de ja vous" moment. The pull of the kite line was forceful, and almost violent. It stopped Randy and prompted him to feel a sense of adrenaline, that crushed him to the very ground he was standing on. He fell that quick and struggled to real some of the kite line in... making it a point not to look up at the sky... death was up in that sky... he remembered that, as Michael returned to grab the kite line. Randy left the kite zone abruptly to return home...

Time passed, amazingly fast. The years went by and Randy did not give the kite incident another thought. Although, there were many other equally perplexing incidents that grabbed his attention... They say energy is not created or destroyed, it is simply transferred (physics 101). And that, Randy believed, was very true. What kind of energy one was talking about was the real question, though. It was a curious thing.... Energy in the form of heat or electricity? Now that sort of energy can be felt or observed with the human eye and the human hand. A hot stove or a bolt of lightning in the sky – fascinating forms of natural energy, yes? no? ... absolutely. Randy came from a pretty big family, with brothers and sisters.... (never a dull moment, growing up) .... The family took a liking to use of Ouija boards, for fun! and tarot card readings in cemeteries, for fun! The thing was, Randy connected to some of the events... during "fun ghost story nights" .... not all of the connections were friendly. There were usually discussions of "Casper the friendly ghost", which resulted in much laughter.... Then there was some incident of "not so friendly entities...".

Randy and his friends grew, finished high school and went their separate ways. Some stayed in touch... while others simply disappeared. There were opportunities for some and others were happy staying "local". Randy always had this inner "manifest destiny compass" that could not be explained with words.... He supposed (to himself) that it was like an energy (not too different from a bolt of lightning or heat) .... An energy that could not be described accurately with words... physics 101, except, in a chapter of science that had not been written or understood, yet.... That summer, after high school graduation – he enrolled in a local University (or should say.... was finally accepted after a long waiting list). The opportunity to study "physics" was there. And that is one of the personal goals he set out to pursue.... the study of "physics' at the college level. There was much too (after all). There was the study of pragmatic, real life elements to physics. The workings of a refrigerator (thermo dynamics), the running of a car engine, the design and architecture of a NYC sky scraper, the fascinating structure of the George Washington Bridge. And that was just the beginning. It was an incredible area of science.... Including other topics like the physical properties of light (at the visible level and non visible level), the essential equations for "space exploration" and the equation for "energy transfer" ....

It was mid-week, and Randy was sitting in the large lecture hall, at University. The class was "genetics 101". Not so easy...in fact, the course lecture was blowing his mind. He sat about five rows back from the front of the lecture stage. And it was a stage, a large performance stage that could be used for a band wind ensemble. Or, in this case, one professor – at a podium. The podium was wired to a sophisticated electronic system. It included a projection screen – for the presentation. It also included a sound system, attached to speakers – located around the large lecture room. The room held around 1,000 seat (on the first level). There was a second level that held around 100 additional seats.... The class was scheduled to begin at the early time of 7 AM. It was 6:40 AM. On the make shift desk, attached to the seat Randy sat at, he placed a notebook and began the process. At the top of the page, was written "lecture 1", the date (September 7th) and the title of the lecture (which corresponded to the curriculum syllabus or was it syllabi? .... he thought, ... Does it really matter? This is going to be a tough class). In the distance, something caught his eye. Near the professor, standing in front of the podium.... looking up onto the stage – at the professor....was a tall, long legged, long haired blonde... he noticed that she was wearing Hollywood style stiletto shoes/heals (was that what the style was called? He wondered.... not that he had any sense of fashion knowledge....). She stood out from the one thousand other students, though. The other students, most of them anyway, were the science geek type.... (which, was cool to him.... Probably not completely true... but they definitely did not have any visual comparison to this girl that was standing in front of the podium... talking with the professor) .... The conversation ended and she turned away from the front room stage... then began to look for a seat. Lecture was beginning in about five minutes (it was 6:55 AM, now).

Randy was staring (maybe not consciously.... He hoped that he wasn't too obvious.... Maybe he was drooling? and that was what caught her attention.... Maybe that was a good thing?) ... She walked calmly with elegance.... and within thirty seconds... was seated right next to Randy. They smiled at each other. She opened her note book and began a similar process to Randy's "note taking"! Randy showed her his notebook. She smiled and giggled! She said "my name is Tina". Randy smiled and introduced himself to Tina. Tina hugged him and kissed him on the cheek. She smiled again and he was lost in her perfume... She continued to talk but he was just floating.... somewhere.... Randy heard an apology for the forwardness (the kiss and hug) ... she said it was a Russian thing! He smiled.... The professor interrupted their conversation and class began...After class, they strolled around the campus. It was enriched with forest, with architectural designs (moderns and historical styles), with distant ball fields, with distant horizon. The air was cool and refreshing – for this was a nice time of year, the autumn season. Tina had some private research to attend to. It was deep in the forest – for an ecology class. She needed to re-visit the "dig" (as they called it) …. She thought, she might have dropped something there – earlier in the week. Randy had no objections. After all, they were together – and that was all that mattered! He did have just one request, though. She smiled and already answered to his gaze. COFFEE! Right? He laughed and said "you know me well". That was it. They stopped near a coffee shop to get some café, then began the walk into the forest….They arrived! And Tina found what she suspected was lost. It was a medallion – or some odd metallic origin – with an infinity symbol on it. They found it while digging in the ground. The ecology class was "fascinating". It was more of an archeology class, if you had asked Tina. Randy seemed to be perplexed. But, it did make sense. The class sectioned off a square, deep in the forest with rope. It was about the length of a football field. And the width, as well. Within the box – the class began their semester long study of the ecological niche. Everything within the square. The plants, the insects, the dirt.... It was there that Tina found the charm. She held it in her hand and looked at it, with Randy. It was dull, and not jewel like....it was more of like a pottery texture.... although there was metallic substance to it.... Oddly, the infinity symbol had a faint glow – a yellowish – green to it... and in the near distance, the dark clouds rolled in... almost in an unnatural way... a sharp bright lightning bolt crossed the sky... as the clouds opened up and dropped heavy rain...

There was no way they could escape the rain. Not a storm that approached them, with such intensity. The storm approached quickly and luckily (for the couple) left the area... similar to the ferocity of a tornado. Tina looked at her charm and was surprised to feel a dull sensation of heat...the heat dissipated rapidly – leaving part of the infinity symbol "charred". The research area, located deep in the forest, was sectioned with a bright red line. The outer perimeter was marked with this line. Interior areas were also sectioned... but, with less obvious looking lines. Tina brought Randy through the area she was responsible for. It was an area near a fascinating birch tree.

Surrounding the tree was a curious looking bamboo patch. Tina's team was digging into and around the birch-bamboo complex. This area – it was located at the far edge of the research. Away from the other groups... and that was a good thing, since Tina had found something extraordinary. She turned to Randy and smirked. That gaze displayed in her eyes, that smirk .... It shook him! it fascinated him. She was a "strong one", a person that had the ability to look outside the box. Then... literally, jump out of the box – turn around, look and then smirk. She was a thinker. Randy knew that she had found something.... But, even for her – it was a curious find. Something that she did not completely understand...at least, not yet. She would find a way to harness the find, though. Perhaps, that was what Randy was there for?

He was thinking all this, he was pondering the qualities of this girl... she then him to the base of the tree. Then said: "I am more than a thinker". Randy's jaw opened wide and was surprised to hear Tina. "you can hear my thoughts?". And, she could – it was her way, her "gift". That ability (they would later find) would prove to help them....as they entered the entrance to the cave. The cave was found during Tina's research dig.... what was in the cave? Tina turned - gazed at Randy – then tugged on his back pack – pulling a flash light out of the sac. She turned it on.... they entered the dark opening....

Chapter 2

Light up the darkness (Bob M.)

It was the strangest thing. Was that even possible, to find what some would call a "passage" to another realm? They existed... those passages. Didn't they? Tina and Randy studied philosophy and Greek literature. There were writings of passages in other parts of the world. Sort of mysterious entries to another place. To another time. The Egyptians, the tribes of South America and Central America. They all were intrigued with it. And now, in north America – on a University campus – Tina found such a passage. Randy followed her into the passage, down a long dirt path. They descended into the darkness – which was lit only by the flash of her light....He followed Tina, it seemed like a long walk – perhaps an hour (it seemed that way – in his mind... then again, when you're with the person that brightens your soul – time does not beat the way time normally beats...does it?) ... as Randy followed directly behind her, in luminescence light, he sort of entered a "day dream"....aware of his surroundings, but content in his "vision". He was appreciative of her....in fact, he really did not know what kind of a man he would have become these days, without her.... She was strong, but approachable. To him, all her love was true and focused – with an incredible precision and accuracy.... Right at his heart and his soul. He felt stronger with her. He felt...his heart was healthier, stronger....and his soul no longer had concrete wall around it...his soul was glowing a bright light...he thought, continued the thought as they walked the path... fire that burns to various degrees of heat/strength...changes in color...where the hottest, most fierce fire changes from the orange to a bluish-white...his soul was bright with intense white-blue. And it was no surprise to him. It was because of her. She made him a better gentleman.... A calmer gentleman, with splashes of champion. She showed him that love can be true, with devotion – fidelity,

understanding and mutual appreciation.....
They arrived at a door. Tina turned to him and
smirked. Her eyes were bright and curious.
She asked if he was day dreaming! He knew,
she could read his mind.... That fascinated
Randy....He really did not have to answer the
question....her smirk said it all. Of course she
knew what he was thinking and they were
happy...their circle made him happy. They
touched lips and kissed. The door was no
ordinary door. It seemed from some other
time and place. Perhaps ancient? But, even
that seemed to be "not right". The texture,
the consistency of the door was not like any
other door they had ever seen before. Not
wood. Not metal. Something different... They
stared into the strange door....

Well, they were moving ahead – moving
forward, excelling into the unknow. That
much they agreed on. Tina and Randy made
no bones about it. The door was there, the
mystery awaited them. It was intimidating.
It was passage into uncharted territory. But,
someone had to move forward. If they didn't
do it, they would regret the chance of a life
time. So, they decided to open the door. The

thing was…. There was no "traditional" door handle. It just wasn't there. This odd, futuristic door – with novel texture, with a dull bronze color was there to open. How to open the door was the question? As they stared at the door, they noticed that the color and shape of the door changed. It was not a dramatic change… but it did change…. gradually, as they stared – the door shape became larger, but stayed rectangular…. The bronze color became a metallic green silver, which was brighter…. Then, the light was quenched, and the door became dull….It was just a theory, but they figured that as the door expanded and became brighter. A bright metallic green… they could press/push it open. So, that was the theory. They decided to test it out. And, as the door reached its climax – timing it, just right… together they pressed forward. Tina and Randy entered the realm together. On the other side, they found they had separated. Randy did not know for sure where Tina disappeared to? He did become immediately aware that he was in the cockpit of a World War II style plane. In the middle of a dog fight. The thing was, he was one with the plane. He was also very clear and calm. He had experience (somehow) with this sort of dogfight. It was in his blood, in his DNA. And he followed his senses....

The airplane was something fierce. It had speed and agility.... The guns were basic, and effective. Within twenty or so minutes the fight had ended. He followed a group of American planes back across ocean. It was fascinating to him. The environment was certainly of another time and place....in the middle of a war against Japanese fighters. The American pilots engaged in a flight pattern across the ocean. Eventually, they reached a United States Aircraft Carrier. And began landing their planes on the flight deck.

Like riding a bike; Randy thought. It was the training, the experience. The flight pattern, the landing was EZ Peezy.... he smirked as he brought the heavy plane onto the flight deck. There was no doubt that he was in a different time. The carrier was vintage, the plane was heavy metal! with history (history to him, innovative for those at that point in time). What had happened? Where was Tina? He wasn't so sure about that. But, he knew that he would find out... soon. The energy was transferred from one point in time to another. The body he found himself in was not so different from his own…. He laughed because he often had those moments… what did they call that? Serendipity? De Ja Vous? A thought that one had been there before, had experienced something in another place, in another time. Was it so crazy, that the door they pushed through verified that this feeling of de ja vous did exist? Leaving the plane, he followed his crew below the flight deck to grab a bite to eat…. He felt at home, and there was nothing unusual. No one suspected anything different from Randy….in fact, his name remained "Randy"… he saw it on his pilots badge. As he ate, the crew was quiet – they were tired from multiple missions in the pacific ocean …. There was a briefing, right in the galley – as they ate. The missions were complete (for now)…. they were sailing back to their home port; Hawaii…..Randy enjoyed the meal. He was tired, but hopeful. In his heart – somehow, he knew that Tina would be there – in Hawaii…. It was a feeling of serendipity, de ja vous. After a bite to eat, in the military styled galley…. Of course, military styled… which meant – cold steel…. No art, no photos, just cold metal, doors, hatches, steel steps, steel walls…. a battle field "container" with various mission readiness. A political deterrent for the world. Just being there was one mission.... If that didn't work... there were multiple capabilities (for that one ship.... there were many others in the battle group...). This ship, was really not a "ship", per se. It was a carrier.... The capabilities were in alignment with air force.... Planes, choppers.... stuff like that.... There were other capabilities... sometimes, capabilities that no one was made aware of... after all, even in the early to mid-1900s... there were technologies! Technological advancement that did not wait for the ferris wheel to complete a turn.... Image the outcomes of previous wars... imagine what would be happening in this war... and, Randy headed to his quarters for sleep... wondering just that... what war were they in... were they really in the pacific, fighting in a world war? Just like that....his life changed, forever..... the third top rack in the barracks styled sleeping quarters was his. He didn't mind.... It was close to the ceiling pipe...the steel.... He didn't mind the odd sound that carried on through the night.... It was sort of refreshing... Randy climbed up the first two rack, then rolled into the top bunk. Top bunk in his division...He would fall asleep...soon... but, wondered if this night would be one of the night's he "sleep walked" or "sleep-talked" ... not a good combination when floating on a piece of steel in the middle of an ocean... he smirked... somehow, he always managed.... As he fell into the dream world...he saw a vision of Tina...in port, Hawaii ... where they were headed. It was her... he knew it... he felt it, with his heart... his soul... (that sort of connection can't be severed easily....) ... She was still her, Tina.... Her hair was flowing, robust...beautiful... her eye brows bushy... her elegance unmatched... yet, she sat alone at this bar... listening to 1920s style band music... drinking something... (Randy hoped it was Rum). He fell asleep...

It was early the next morning when he woke. The ship was sailing smoothly through calm seas. That was a good thing. Out there, in the deep ocean... it was never that smooth. Not usually...yeah... that was the thing about the ocean... mother nature could be fierce.... more often than less often.... Randy quickly realized it was a Saturday morning. He knew because the cleaning parties were being assembled and the weekly cleaning of the barracks was happening... he could smell the bleach. He climbed down the bunk wall and made his way to the head. The showers were awful... but, he was clean after five minutes. Clean shave, clean skin.... Clean heart... At the galley as short briefing took place... the ship was pulling into port that night, and they were happy to hear it. The first stop in port was to the "base club". It was actually located across the way from Pearl harbor naval station. A place called Hickam airforce base, Hawaii. The crew deserved it...and they would enjoy some entertainment that first night – at the club.... As the ship pulled into port, later that evening.... The ropes secured the floating steel.... It was quit amazing to see.... The procedure to secure the ship was no joke.... Quite a process.... Anyway, Randy followed the other pilots to the club that night...

Inside the base club there was a live band playing 1920s style music. His favorite was the saxophone solos with the romantic verses.... Something special was found in the melody of this genre... He sat at the bar and wondered how he knew so much about music genres...he didn't study much of it… yet, it was there…from another time and place – perhaps… yes? no? then, he wondered more about the University dig…the door Tina had stumbled upon… and where he found himself… was it really so hard to believe? That transfer of energy to different places in time and place…. Some call it de ja vous… serendipity… or just this familiarity with an environment? He sipped his rum and juice….it was good, like candy. As before, in his visions…. The elegant lady…. With the rose clip in her hair… appeared! she was at the bar, but was being approached by some guy… Randy turned to her and quickly left his seat to approach the guy that was aggressively grabbing her…. There wasn't much thought….as before (in his dreams) …. his fist made its way to the side of this guy's jar (effectively, efficiently) … which resulted in his hand releasing her dress… and, as before (in his dreams) … She grabbed his arm, knowing exactly who he was! She escorted him away from the bar…. to her room… Their eyes widened and smirks appeared on both their faces… they knew!

In her room, Tina did not hesitate one moment. She grabbed Randy and kissed him. They talked. [was it so hard to believe... there were many people that experienced the serendipity, the de ja vous in their lives... perhaps it was just the right energy being sent to different places in time; where a familiarity with one another existed. Randy was intrigued by Tina's conversation. She was transferred to this place in time, on the Naval base – Pearl Harbor, Hawaii! A tropical climate, lots of pineapples, and sunny beaches. She loved Hawaii. Of course, the time in history was not ideal. It had been attacked by the Japanese. Even decades, upon decades after the attack – some structures for buildings remained. The walls of new buildings were built behind the bullet ridden walls of the pearl harbor attack....]

The Hawaii beach was magnificent. Tina brought Randy to the seashore – for a walk. They talked more.... The sun was setting, and they observed the shine of sun beams on the tropical waters surface. It seemed too good to be true (Tina whispered to Randy). They smiled at each other, continuing their walk along the moist sand. The sun light was gone and it was dark. Tina had been on the island during Randy's piloting and travel through the pacific-ocean.... During that time, she took notes. Observations, so to speak.... She called the observations: "oddities" or "reflective-events". It perplexed her.... For example, what seemed normal was no longer normal. In the world they traveled from, things were aligned with natural order... the laws of nature. Here, in this place – on this island... the history was correct.... The music they heard fit the time and place. The people, events fit the history.... But in a reflective manner. In the distance they heard what seemed like howls... beast-like howls... Tina smirked and offered Randy a place to sleep – her room. It wasn't much, but the location was great. Breakfast near the beach, the fresh ocean breeze each morning... very nice! The howls continued, and seemed to be getting closer to them.... A moon appeared in the sky – as if it was artificially placed into a space.... Tina called it an "oddity". There was something about this place that was not right, was not natural. The place was a rip in time... perhaps a place forgotten, perhaps a place that was trapped....sort of squeezed in between present day, past day and present day.... A reflection of what should be. A reflection of what shouldn't be... It was perplexing to both Tina and Randy.... They decided to call it a night, and they slept...The air was cleaner in Hawaii. They woke, together – as a refreshing pacific-ocean breeze breeched the room. The air was fresh ocean scent, with a newness to the environment. After all, they had recently left an older world – somehow, went back to a younger environment. The schedule for the morning was simple. They had nothing scheduled. Just time together! Randy spoke of the air quality in new jersey. He said it was okay, but not ocean like. He missed the ocean air quality. Growing up on Long Island, that was something people enjoyed... air quality. Tina smiled and realized that although they were in a different time and place... it was if they knew each-other, in another life. Soul mates – that is something that can not be faked. It was a feeling, a feeling of familiarity... The conversation led to a simple plan. Randy didn't like it... he needed to stay close to the base, but eventually agreed with Tina. They were to board a plane that night and head back to the University... which, would be a long plane ride back to Long Island, New York... So, that night – they boarded a MAC flight from the air force base. It was a large military aircraft that made its way... back to Mitchell field, Long Island...

The flight was smooth, but lengthy. Not so bad, but very lengthy.... They slept some of the way... and talked during some other parts of the flight. After leaving the airport, in a taxi – they quickly realized that everything had changed. Life's like that sometimes. You leave for a period of time, and upon return – nothing is as it was. Sometimes that is a good thing. Other times, it seems like not such a good thing (in the short run) ... If only they possessed a crystal ball. Hugh? Wouldn't that have been helpful in this situation, or in any other situation.... Tina looked at Randy with a cute grin. A grin that pierced his inner thoughts and bright soul. There wasn't much more to say. They were in tune with each other. That much they knew. As far as everything else, they would soon find out....

Chapter 3

Back at the University, they found a fresh campus. Newly built, and designed to nurture learning. Free of hardcore politics, far right or far left idealism. And this is the way it is. The curriculum presented by the professors were approved by the faculty champions. Proposals for some changes were often heard, but changes rarely were entertained.... Unless, of course – there was a "technological break-through". In those cases – the faculty quickly included the literature to the curriculum. Some examples of technological break-throughs included the discovery DNA, RNA, mRNA. The blue print for life as we knew it. Tina and Randy giggled and wondered if travel through time would be approved for changing a college curriculum?

They found a student dorm to sleep in. Tina knew of it, and they researched – or should say scoped it out to see if it was "available". It was. The campus was quiet – which meant, they came at a perfect time. Perhaps a semester break, a holiday... they really weren't sure. But, at least it bought them some time to explore the ecology site, the tunnel that put them here – in this place, in this time.

In the dorm, the room they found was cozy. Randy and Tina showered – together. Something was always comforting and peaceful, together.... They sat at a dinette style table and ate some ramon noodles together. Conversation was interesting to Randy. You see, although Tina had just met Randy (not too long ago), he sensed (a seventh sense) that she knew of him. So, he asked her – straight up. Randy said to her, I spent most of my life trying to stay "low-key" – about certain things. Things that are of another world, perhaps another place and time. Some things that I understand, other things that fascinate me. So, I am curious – How did you find me? Tina looked at Randy "wide eyed" ...It was mutual, though. They had found each other. They thought of some physics, just deep theories... some of it was difficult to follow. She did not struggle though. Randy admired that kind of brilliance. He was able to process, understand the theories. That was always part of the battle. But, she did more... She was able to process the theories and continue on. She developed pragmatic questions... a hypothesis.... As Randy suspected, she found a way to get back – to the place and time they had left. He was happy to know she was good. She was with him...... there had been too many times he found himself on "divergent paths" with people. People that seemed good, but were not. He had no problem changing direction when the sense of divergency was even suspected. No problem changing direction. He could change in a week, in a day, in an hour. Depending on the situation. She was okay though.... True to the core. Reasonable. Easy to understand. He admired that sort of personality. Strong minded, intelligent...yet, gentle and loving with a rational sense of goals.

It was dark. Too dark. The place Tina and Randy were in... was not right. It seemed, different to them? Looking out the window, they searched for stars. They searched for a moon. Nothing. Just darkness. Another thing that was odd. There were no sounds in the night. No crickets, no night noise. It just seemed odd to Tina. Even the shadows were different. And with those thoughts, they decided to get some sleep. Tina woke in the middle of the night. At the far corner of the room – a shadow figure moved. In the corner of the room, Tina thought she observed the glow of eyes. She woke Randy and pointed in the direction of the glow. By the time he got his night eye sight – the shadow had vanished from the room. They couldn't sleep much after that incident. So, they talked. the air was different and what they figured was that they theoretically entered some sort of a rip in time. Randy thought about it. The unit he was assigned to over the pacific seemed like a crew of lost souls. Something with the aircraft he flew also seemed odd. It was like he was flying over the pacific with a group of corpses. Come to think of it …. he didn't recall much conversation… and in the galley, the lights were so dim… it was if the crew had turned into an image… tina sat up in bed, found lip gloss. It had a scent of berry. It had the clear appearance, with sparkles on her lips. She squinted at Randy, in a seductive way. He didn't need instructions... well, whatever had happened to them... they were sure of the fact that their love was hot and pure. The next morning, Tina and Randy took a stroll around campus. The University was newly built, was designed with basic infrastructure. The land was familiar to them. The buildings on campus were not completely familiar. There were less buildings and the structures were basic construct. Of course, they found a place to get a cup of coffee. They sat in the campus café and continued the discussion that surrounded the theory of "ghosts over the pacific". It was something that was entirely possible. Randy insisted that there were many accounts of tragic events through history. Events that were "sudden", in terms of loss of life. That much tragedy in a short time, could most definitely create a "ghost entity". And Randy shook his body as if getting the chills from sudden onset of the kung flu. Imagine that, he flew alongside these ghost pilots.... It seemed so real.... Then of course, he was starting to wonder what "reality" actual was? Maybe, perhaps they were all dead and this was some kind of purgatory. Ya know, he was Catholic (back in his time) and purgatory is a real place for those Catholics. Hell (no pun intended), a poet from the 1300s even wrote about the levels of hell, purgatory and heaven...... Dante was his name (if he remembered correctly....) Tina sipped her coffee, paused and silence filled the café.... She smiled at Randy... then spoke: "so, did you like the berry lip gloss?". Randy turned his worries into a smirk... then they laughed... she was a good soul... he was thankful for that.... If he had to be lost somewhere, at least he was with Tina.

The University was a self-sustainable campus. Located, essentially, in a forest. The forest was not too far from the Long Island sound – a body of water that was part of the Atlantic-ocean. It separated Connecticut from Long Island, New York. The energy to power the lights, mechanics, experiments, lecture halls, ... was sourced by water. A hydro-electric station. The station was fenced. No entry, unless you were authorized. The engineer, named jake, entered the facility. He was tall, heavy, with a beard. His eyes were dark... too dark. His walk was hunched and everything around him seemed to grow dark, as he passed. Once inside the energy station, he took an elevator down to the basement – and beyond. At the greatest depth of the University was an odd looking – ancient looking boiler. What fueled this boiler was a mystery. It had been there, even before Jake had arrived...Jake sat down, in his warm office. The boiler was heating the very large room. There were some guests this day. But, first he fed his two devil dogs. Dovers – very loyal, very feisty, very viscous! They ate two slabs of raw meat, Jake had thrown across the room. He heard snarls and growls as they ate the raw beef. Jake was trying to remember if the meat was of animal origin or if it was left over from his last human kill. He really wasn't sure. It didn't matter. He killed for sport, he murdered for fun. At first out of necessity, to fuel the boiler. Then, just for the hell of it. The visitors were two women and a guy called Barry. Very rough looking. Rotten teeth for the guy... The women were sort of elegant, in a strange way. Maybe at first glance. Then, after conversation – it was clear they were of goon-like origin. Perfect chess pieces for the next string of murders.... Jake grinned at the group and offered some hard liquor. They sat and drank the booze. The University was thriving, the campus was full of students and faculty. The surrounding towns benefitted from the University endeavors. The local towns had plenty of potential victims.... But, this was a strange place. Not the everyday life people recognized.... Even Jake hadn't completely figured out where he was; where they were.... But he served what some would call "evil". He served all he knew to serve, since he had arrived. It was a mutual relationship. He murdered or had victims murdered.... The energy was fed into the boiler.... And the energy was harnessed for the University, which kept the "realm" (or where ever they were at) going..... It was often dark in this realm, it was a realm, and alternative zone – a place in time that was here and there – or perhaps did not exist, at all.... Jake did not really care to think about it. He just wanted to feed his dogs, keep the fires hot and continue to kill for sport....The group left the boiler room, with their explicit instruction to carry out the next set of killings.... The bodies would be brought back to Jake within a week. The bodies would be torn apart to get at the energy needed to fuel the boiler. Within the heart, within the deepest chamber – two things were certain…. A pace maker that continued to beat the heart and the energy of the soul… it was this energy that was needed….

Chapter 4

The boiler was running hot. The flame inside this huge rusty iron container was deep white, bluish and surrounded with orange lights. The massive amount of heat generated from this mechanism was enough to heat the entire room. Jim, the engineer, did not seem to mind the excessive amount of heat. In fact, he and his dogs, sort of took a liking to it. Even though the heat was high enough to melt human skin off the bones and underlying flesh. Perhaps, Jim and his dogs were not of this world. Perhaps no one in this time and place was of this world. Perhaps it was just a "staging area". A holding area for future transport. Some would go further to the depths of hell. Others, perhaps, would rise to a cooler level... in a brighter realm of purgatory... It was just a theory by Jim. Either way, he did not give a shit. He murdered for sport so he could keep the realm at a balance – after feeding the burner with victims. Some, of course, would find its way to his dover dogs... They enjoyed the human flesh. Jim didn't eat much. He liked the hard liquor. Ironically, the "red devil drink". A mixture of tomato juice, a raw egg (the devil's eye) and seven mixed liquors. That kept him going. Occasionally, he ordered a pizza from the campus pizzeria! That was all he really needed. That and instructions to the next set of victims....

The campus opened once again. It was alive with groups of students. Randy and Tina could see the groups of students strolling around campus with their books, their backpacks, and intensity. The way they walked. With purpose. From one building to the next, ready for a lecture. Ready for laboratory. Ready for a study session, etc. Although, Tina noticed that something was not right here. She pointed to the sky. Didn't the sky seem darker than usual? It sort of reminded her of an approaching snow storm. The sky was gray and in some parts, not very light... But, very dark grey. In the distance, flashes of light caught their attention. Lightning?

Snow? Strange. Maybe, nothing of the sort. Perhaps, just a coincidence? The people. They seemed... different. Not much conversation? In fact, yes – there was no conversation. The "human elements" were missing, in this place and time. Randy thought of the group of military jet fighters. After he landed on the Navy aircraft carrier....and made his way to the mess hall, for chow. He was thinking back to his seat. His surroundings. No talking...not really. As if, holograms? Ghost artifacts? Is that what they would call it? He wasn't sure. But, this campus also reminded him of some sort of ghost artifact. A place and time that was here. But, was not really here... if that made any sense. Tina looked at Randy with concern. She knew, that they were certainly on to something.... The place they were in was of another era.... Another time, around the early 1900s. The place was here, but certain parts of it.... well. defied the basic laws and principles of physics; of biology; of chemistry; of nature.

They visited the campus perimeter. It had changed, and they needed to discover the approximate place of the "cave". The dig site, that led to the cave. The forest was not as open as they had hoped for. It was full of brush, plants, rocks and more trees.... over the years, the campus grounds went through changes. Mostly, architectural changes. But, the brush and trees were also part of the routine university maintenance. Randy always wondered where some of the large stones came from. Perhaps the large rocks were trucked in from the northern Adirondack region. Either way, it was fascinating to observe. There weren't many paths – as they made their way through the forest. The forest, it seemed.... Magical to the explorers. Although, the adventure was not a vacation. The exploration through the trees and brush was more a life saving necessity. The sense to adventure among the unknown was in their blood. They knew it. Perhaps, that was one of the unspoken energy they felt for each other (right from the beginning). The energy was felt between Randy and Tina. He followed her, as she marched forward. She believed the cave was near. And it was! They found the opening.... Which, had been there long before the University was built. Long before man and woman had come to be. Or, They should say long before this place existed? What was this place they had stumbled upon, anyway? Tina did not think that the place had good energy. The place they found themselves in, it had a sort of evil entity to it. A darkness. In fact, Tina couldn't recall when she saw the bright sunlight since they arrived. There was a light in the sky. Yes? it was different... The energy from the "sun" was quenched. Dark.

The mechanic met with his group, another productive "talk meeting". The mechanic, Jim – he was tired of the talk. He wanted to murder. It was a sport to him. He needed to feed his dogs. He felt the energy waning. The burner was losing light. Was losing heat. Jim needed to fuel it with the next set of victims. He smirked in a most awkward way. Even his group of goons felt uncomfortable.... Except for one lady. Was she a lady? Not really. One dark entity stood there smiling back at the mechanic. She cackled. A stupid attempt at laughter. Not that it mattered to her. She was happy as a pig in shit. Surrounded by shit. The two caught each-other's eyes. She spoke. She knew of two that arrived in this place. Somehow, they arrived and they were in the university forest, trying to get back……. The mechanic was intrigued. He knew that if it were true. This kind of energy would fuel the burner and his dogs for a significant amount of time. Since, their energy was intense and pure. Very bright…

The dark, red eyed mechanic (or whatever he was) motioned the end of the meeting. The group left, with an urgency to comb the university for Tina and Randy. And they would find them, efficiently – they had their ways of achieving a hunt. Deep in the forest, a group of students made their way past the cave….not realizing that the cave was there. Or, that Tina and Randy were in it. Tina had a feeling. A gut feeling that something wasn't right. Randy laughed, and said – of course! We are trapped somewhere, someplace, some time? Tina looked concerned. No, it is not that. The evolutionary sense, a feeling… That they were being hunted. Randy felt it now. She was right. Counter measures. He smirked. Truth is, there was more to who he was. More than Tina knew. Why was he taking some sort of excitement to a counter measure? Yeah, he liked it. And, so they hid behind a big pine tree. Maybe it was a hybrid tree. It could have been oak. Tina said, really? You are debating with me about the kind of tree we are hiding behind... when we are being hunted by some savage devil zombies! She paused, then laughed.... Well, it is a good way to keep the spirits light! And it was, of course. He knew it.... It was his way of lightning the situation... even though, the situation was not a good one. It was getting dark in the forest when the group of "devil zombies" approached.... Randy and Tina ducked behind the large oak/pine tree. Luckily, they were positioned on higher ground. The terrain was hilly and there many trees, lots of brush... as the group passed, Tina whispered in Randy's ear. Do you see the red light, coming from their eyes? Randy could see the evil. They could feel the evil as it passed through the forest. Tina whispered... "we should follow". And, that is what they did. At a distance, they could see the evil approach the group of students. There were screams, and "crunching" of forest twigs, sticks, branches...brush... or was that sound human bones being "snapped". They weren't sure, but decided to head back to the campus room....[not that they didn't want to help, they did. It was just that the people here did not see "alive" and they did not want to become "dead" ... they needed to get back to the cave... eventually, hopefully.... if they were lucky enough to figure out the way back home...]. In the campus room, they locked the door, windows and slid furniture against the door. Tina was visibly shaken. Randy was too... although, he still seemed to like the "counter measures" to combat this evil. He smirked... and asked Tina if she had any knives?

The campus was busy that day. Tina and Randy walked along the paths, grabbed a cup of coffee along the way. They were exploring.... Trying to see what was really happening in this realm. In this place. In this time. At first glance, the environment seemed okay. The people seemed okay. However, upon careful observation, they noticed some oddities.... some strangeness to the surroundings. The air, the trees, the surroundings.... Were greyish. The clarity of a brisk morning was not there. There was something missing. In the distance, Tina could see something that caught her eye – in a flash. The students that were standing around, in a circle... they were laughing...

and in a quick second of time, their smiles extended past their cheek bones to their ears. A dark space in their heads revealed sharp beastlike teeth. Then the appearance of each student returned to normal. Something was not right with this place. And it was hidden. But, isn't that usually the case? The creation of some societal elements, populations of people with a common culture – a culture of evil. And, once created – they blended in – like the ability of a lizard to hide in and around brush. The air was different to. The breeze carried with it, stagnant stale-like wind. It was not refreshing. To breath in a cool ocean breeze or the scent of a forest is "refreshing". This air was the opposite of that. Tina and Randy continued their walk through the campus, when they were approached by a lady. A student with long shiny hair. A gorgeous brunette with long eye lashes, long legs – very tall – very beautiful. Her eyes glistened, with a shine that did not belong in this place. There was almost a bright glow coming from her body. Randy thought he saw this brightness, among the grey environment. She was sharp – very witty and to the point. She introduced herself as "Rebecca". Her style was something different, much different than this place and time. She did not have the typical college student, relaxed clothes style. Nor did she show a style of what they thought was the early 1900s. No, she had what some would call "the modern style". Long legs, tall – probably close to 5 feet 10 inches or possible 6 feet tall. Randy wasn't to sure since her stiletto heal added a few inches. Rebecca smiled as she made deep eye contact with Randy. Tina jabbed Randy's ribs with her elbow. A forceful elbow, and Randy expelled air into the grey stagnant environment. Tina was also to the point. Tina was also very sharp. And very protective of what was hers. She said "who the hell are you" and what do you want from us? Rebecca slowly released her gaze from Randy. Then directed her attention to Tina....

Chapter 5

Rebecca advised to leave the campus. It wasn't safe to talk in this area. There was too much darkness. And this was true. The dark figures that strolled along the University paths were there – but, not really there. She spoke of remnants of "dark matter". They were trapped in what was explained as a temporary holding area. They had some viability, some sort of energy.... But, very gray.... Borderline, dark and with an affinity for darkness... Rebecca continued her conversation with Tina and Randy – as they walked through the campus, reaching the outer perimeter. There, at the perimeter, was a train station. Rebecca sat on the train station bench, then unzipped.... Her back pack. She pulled out a pair of sneakers. The sneakers looked more comfortable to walk in, than the stiletto shoes she was currently wearing. Tina asked where they were going? She was sure, as she heard the train approach the station. Passengers got off the train, and Randy noticed they too were of a "dark energy". Randy cringed and felt the hair on his neck stand up. Something was not right with this place. Rebecca placed her heels into the backpack, zipped it and continued to walk. They left the campus perimeter, passing lost souls...as they got off the train. The souls did not speak, they just followed...almost like some scene from a really good zombie movie [Randy thought]. It was a nice University campus, perfect for nurturing growth. Although, this place in this time – was not so nurturing. It was stagnant, like stale water. As they left the campus, Tina noticed the grey became white light. The surroundings seemed brighter. It was true, the trees were greener – the air was fresher.

Within fifteen minutes of the outer University campus perimeter, they found a local restaurant. Rebecca knew it well. Tina and Randy knew it as a really good Japanese restaurant [from their time and place]. It was still a pretty good restaurant. They sat and ordered their meals. As they ate together, it was apparent to Tina that this "Rebecca" was different from the other souls. They listened to Rebecca speak to the time and place. At least, what was the "University campus". Sort of a temporary staging area. The campus was full of "zombies". Rebecca was of a heavenly origin. Perhaps, less than heavenly.... Perhaps in a level of "purgatory", where she was given a mission. Upon completion of her "mission", she would have a chance to levitate to the heavens [where ever that was, whatever that was... because, sometimes "Heaven is a place on Earth"]. Rebecca was aware of the boiler room, the engineer, the fuel for the boiler... and so on and so forth...... she continued to enlighten Tina and Randy with the evil that existed.... The next step was to target the evil and destroy this dark matter. And, they would in fact do that.... it started with the understanding of what fueled this evil entity... It was a very tough reality. Evolution, lineages of species, trees of divergence.... It was just what was, what had been and what continues to be. The lineage of evil went back as far as Rebecca could remember.... She was just a servant, a soul with a mission. There was more to the story. Wasn't that usually the case? Of course. The time and space were immense. Greater than what she could imagine. Greater than what most people could imagine. Unless, of course, a soul was granted a gift. The gift of "awareness". Or, more like a cure. Randy sat quietly and wished he never had the cure [he meant, the gift]. Sometimes, ignorance really is bliss. What was that saying? [Randy thought, as Rebecca continued to talk....]. Oh, yeah – that was it... "be careful what you wish for.... You just might get it]. So, some how and with God's grace (they imagined) – these two, these three souls crossed a path together. And, would be together – forever. You see, forever is not just the "years" we create on Earth. Forever, is inclusive of what some would call the "after life". We continue on.... we continue to propel into other realms of adventure... other realms of challenges, and here they were – the realm of a University that was fueled by a hot boiler.... led by an evil engineer that just wanted to feed his dogs... The plan was not too difficult. Sort of like football. The team could know exactly what the play was. Exactly, the strategy of the play. That would be okay.... that did not mean the play could be stopped. Run the ball up the middle in what was termed "a dive". Do it and know it. But, can you stop it? Run full speed into a body in an open tackle, and then one understands by that logic. Know the play, but can you stop the play? Anyway, Randy was deep in thought as Rebecca was questioned by Tina... They decided to go back to the University dormitory. Rebecca invited them. It was their ticket to what would come next....

Her dormitory was elegant, sophisticated. It seemed to be very classy for a student. As if she were from another place and time. And, she was from somewhere else. Rebecca offered Tina and Randy some hot tea. The space was limited, yet optimal. They sat at a round table. Randy liked to lighten the situation. He joked, with the table analogy.... This is the nights round table? They smirked... [Randy felt outnumbered, lady to gentleman... he smirked too and giggled, it was cute] ... a kitchen area, a hot plate, a dorm refrigerator/ freezer. And a bed. The lightning was dim, yet elegant. Rebecca explained that the boiler was located in the depths of the University. It would be guarded by viscous dogs. Dover man pinchers – was that the right breed of dog? Evil?

these dogs, anyway – were in fact evil. Aces to the engineer. They guarded the fire around the clock. The engineer, Jim, spent most of his time there too. But, when he left the area – the dogs stayed....The situation was fascinating to Tina and Randy. How was it possible that they made their way to this place? Rebecca shed some light into the situation. It was possible that something traumatic happened. She asked Tina if something had happened. Tina and Randy thought that maybe something did happen.... They remember travelling into a dark cave, then there was a "transfer of energy" (if that was the correct way to put it?).

The sun set outside the elegant styled dorm they were in. They had just finished a simple pasta dinner with meat balls...washing it down with wine. The lights were dim, and the reflection of some distant light could be seen at the edge of the window. It was a bright luminescent light that was being generated in the campus forest. It was a curious site. Brighter than the brightness of a still full moon, on a calm night. The souls were connected. They agreed to hop on the train, in the early morning. Rebecca needed to show

Tina and Randy something in the city. They would travel by train to the "city". In the city, there was a place called "China town". In this part of the city, they would meet Rebecca's contact. A soul from another time and place. This China town place would offer some things that would be needed. That would be needed, as they would eventually approach the evil campus entity... the warm boiler that fueled the place and time they were in.... Rebecca grabbed Tina's hand, gently. Then kissed her temple and ear. Randy nibbled on Tina's other ear. They made their way to the bed and snuggled through the night; loving each other....The sun shined through the window, reflecting bright light into the dormitory room. Randy was up, making coffee for Rebecca and Tina. They showered and were now ready to travel into the city, via train.... As they walked through the campus forest, following the path... there was a quiet, almost eerie feeling that surrounded them. They could not hear the sounds of any birds. Not like before. And the air was different. Not just stagnant. Randy thought it was a "calm before a fierce storm". It was possible. What wasn't possible in this place? {as Tina and Rebecca spoke, Randy was thinking... remembering that time he was in a tornado storm.... the environment here in this University... this place/time reminded him of the tornado storm.... He was in Chicago, in a barracks.... brick and windows.... the pressure surrounding them changed, suddenly.... The awareness that something was not right ensued everyone's mind.... It was a significant change in the environment, the air pressure.... and it was followed with every window getting blown into the main barracks...... the tornado dropped, hitting every structure in its path.... except where they were...... Randy looked around as Tina and Rebecca walked next to him....

He looked up and wondered if a tornado was about to drop on them?} ....

Train To China Town

They made it to the modest train station. The tracks ran through the outer edge of the University property. It had been a nice walk through the forest, following a distinct path. The path seemed fresh, like it was "new". Of course, what would that mean in a place like this? Where time was there...sort of? The sun, or what seemed to be the sun, did rise each morning. And the moon followed in the evening, or so it did seem that way.... The train arrived and they boarded it. The train left, and they sat pleasantly as it moved off the University campus. The group was westbound, to the city. Leaving the suburbs and entering the city would take anywhere from forty minutes to an hour. Depending on the amount of stops in between. There were express trains that did not stop so often between the suburbs and city life. The people on the train, the surrounding air, the environment located around the train tracks....did not seem kosher. The surroundings seemed odd. Seemed tainted. Randy mentioned it to Rebecca. She smiled and replied, you are correct. Is anything what it should be here? We are, in fact, in a level between present day and .... well, she left it at that. Randy was perplexed and squeezed Tina's hand. When Tina and Randy were transported from the present-day University dig site, to Pearl Harbor.... where did they transport to? And where ever this place was.... what sort of bridge was it leading to? A battle of good verse evil... Randy stated to Tina.... Rebecca smiled again....no, smirked, in a kind way.... A pleasant way.... She was good.... They sensed that. Rebecca calmed their thoughts by saying that when they reach "China Town" ... things will become clearer...... okay? The train pulled into the city station. They were now underground in a network of subway train cars. Tina and Randy followed Rebecca to the train and within twenty minutes (what seemed twenty minutes), they arrived in China Town.

Randy knew of "China Town". He visited the area many times. This place was different. It was not much of a surprise to Tina and Randy, though. Similar to the University, the surrounding environment was darker.... Sort of like a dim light, compared to the intensity of a stronger watt light bulb. The people were there, but seemed more like going through the motions. Not much thought, just walking around with blank eyes, empty smiles, dull and uncoordinated movements. It was bizarre, but not a surprise to the group. Rebecca led the way into a funeral parlor. Her contact owned the parlor. It was of Chinese origin. And, as they made their way through the home.... A service was happening. It was near the end, and so, they took seats at the back of the room. In front of the room, there was a group placing folded paper notes into a furnace. The furnace was open and vented to the ceiling. As the notes burned, the ashes made way up.... to the heavens (the symbolism). This was fascinating to Randy and Tina. Different from a Christian and Catholic funeral service....The people left for the night and Rebecca introduced Tina and Randy to Angie. She was an elderly looking lady, with fitness and energy. Angie brought the group to the roof of her funeral parlor.... Where rooftop furniture was neatly arranged. They sat and shared a bottle of table wine. Remarkably tasty for this place, for this time, for wherever this place and time was.... Angie did shed light on the situation. And it was what was suspected, since the arrival in Hawaii. They were, in fact, between the present day (where Tina and Randy traveled from) and the past (early 1900s to mid-1900s). Sort of a "staging area", dimensional and required for some energy, not all energy. Most, leave their time and energy is not lost or gained....it merely is transferred along dimensions, and does make its way into the soul of others. This could be good (most hoped) .... And this "process" could also be "bad" (for the darker enriched souls…. If that was what they had? Souls?) …

It was a nice evening and they made their way back to the train and to the University…. not before collecting some much-needed tools. On the train ride back to the University, Randy chuckled (in a worrisome way, in a frightened way). He continued to speak…. the classic good versus evil story, yes? no? of course? Wonderful! why not. Rebecca smiled in an understanding way. She comforted Tina and Randy. We have the right tools, now. The tools were of ancient Chinese culture. She held the tools in a medium sized cloth bag. Within the bag were essential tools to combat the evil that existed at the University. They would travel, together and confront evil in the hot basement of the University. They would be ready for evil dog attacks. They would be ready for evil tricks. They would be ready to defeat such evil, then return home…. but, first they decided to rest in Rebecca's dorm…. it was late, they were tired and needed some rest.

Final fight....

The University ground was quite spectacular. The plants, trees, shrubs and architecture was maintained by the ground crew. The lead engineer, Jake was proficient. He always had a liking to the field he was in. The boiler, the furnace.... Whatever, you chose to call it was the thing that kept him in this place, this time. Jake was well aware of the mystery behind the heat. The boiler was located deep in the basement of the biological science building, right in the center of the University. Surrounded by Spanish style architecture, and ample space to walk around....to talk, to think, to eat, to just stroll along.... The University setting was quite a sight to see. A nice place to spend four to five years. Normal years, or in this place and time.... Perhaps, normal was not recorded as "normal time". Jake blended into the University community. It's not like he blended in a way to be mistaken for a student or a professor. He was blended in to be a crew member. A good coat, a reasonable shirt that appeared clean. He was a "yes man". A minion, or that was what he wanted to present. When he left the grounds, and traveled to the basement....his appearance changed. His clean shirt was removed an placed neatly outside the hot room. As he entered the boiler room, his appearance changed – to a grotesque bone like entity.... A creature of hell. If hell existed, if all the literature was accurate.... He was representing "hell". But, most common people knew that "hell" did not have to be something supernatural.... It did not have to be unreachable. You see, hell (as most knew of it) did in fact exist in every day life. And, the groups that went on doing what they do.... Fueling the furnace of hell.... did not know it. Did not believe it. In fact, the groups believed they were performing angelic acts of kindness... or justified acts in not such a kind way.... But it was okay, because they were combating what they deemed "evil" ....

There was no television at this time and place. Not that it was needed. There was plenty of music. Jake enjoyed a simple record player. With an ample collection of records.... A variety of music genres was always playing in the 100+ temperature environment. Jake grabbed his poison, rum. Sat down next to the burner and listened to some early 1900s music. He enjoyed the rum, but thought the room temperature was too cool. He needed to fuel the furnace to increase the temperature.... The flame was dwindling.... First, the rum was being gulps in massive quantities.... His dogs sat next to his chair, content by his side. He was thinking. A scary process for Jake. He was the opposite of the age old saying: "hear no evil, see no evil, speak no evil" .... he wondered why that saying didn't have in it: "think no evil". That should have been included, no? yes? perhaps it was inferred, extrapolated? Perhaps not? The dogs were getting hungry, the furnace flame was losing its intensity.... Jake was craving a kill. Where and who would he target? His minion killed enough for him, for his dogs, for his furnace…. however, Jake was craving a kill of his own! Jake continued to "think". The furnace. Where did it vent to? It was no ordinary furnace. This thing had been around for quite some time. Longer than Jakes time, longer than he really knew…. It was similar to an area of study that reflected on things we did not know. Yes, although Jake was not the "professor", he was schooled in life and with his acquired knowledge over the years…. One could call him an evil contender… in the area of philosophy…. Existential philosophy.

Chapter 6

Rebecca woke with Randy. They made some coffee, together. Tina woke to aroma of the freshly brewed coffee. It would be a big day. They ate breakfast, drank coffee and reflected on their visit to China Town. Tonight, they would visit the University biology building and confront the evil entity that existed for far too long. The evil entity would be destroyed, tonight. At least, that was Rebecca's theory. They laughed. They all knew very well and good... that theories were better when motioned to be "a practical application". Their spirits were bright, their hope was strong and they had some spiritual guidance. That was always helpful. The reactor, or whatever it was.... Seemed to be fueled by some sort of cold energy.... And the energy was supporting the current place and time.... Rebecca had been there for some time, and was knowledgeable about the way the energy could transport... she learned it from her contacts in China town.... The group huddled around the energy and simply decided to just enter the transport medium, with faith. Rebecca had seen things, people transported – in her time there. They looked at the technical dash board, with settings.... the time for return entered into the system, not with number, but with an item from Tina. A piece of jewelry. She supposed that the artifact registered or "identified" who they were... place and time. Rebecca believed that.... And so, they entered the bright cold, blue energy.... within a flash of light, within the action potential of an electrical signal along a human nerve.... they returned to the University. Randy, Tina and Rebecca found themselves in the cave at the University dig site. They gingerly walked through the tunnel and found the University classmates digging... same place and time.... With no gap in dimensional coordinates! (Randy felt fascinated by what had just happened, but more intrigued by the fact that all the surrounding people went about their activities as usual! not one person, including the professor, suspected anything!). It would be better to wait until evening. When the sun set and the campus was quiet, they would make their way to the biology building. The day was warm and calm. A nice day to walk along the campus paths. The group rented bikes for the day and explored. The campus had ample grounds for exploration. And, so, that is what the group did. Following the windy and hilly cement bike paths through the forest was refreshing. They made their way through the main campus and eventually found a hidden research facility. It was the marine biology laboratory. Most lectures were given on the main part of campus. While, hidden deep in the forest…. A research lab existed…. They drove around the side of the research building, then hid their bikes behind a large oak tree. The trees in this part of the forest were fascinating! There were many oaks, birch trees…. areas of thick bamboo and some pine trees. A very diverse forest. One of the side doors was left open, and Rebecca quickly entered. The lab seemed empty at this time. Bizarre, but lucky for them. Perhaps, there was a lecture for marine biology happening in the main campus lecture hall. And, this lab would be full much later in the day…. With researcher, exploring the mysteries of deep ocean life.

There was something odd, though. Inside the lab, there seemed to be an odd feeling. Something was not right with the lighting in the lab. Come to think of it, other things were not right. There was a strange sound coming from the back of the room.... Tina, Randy and Rebecca approached....As the group got closer to the strange noise, it became clear to them that there was an energy. An energy that was similar to static electricity (that was a theory). They could, in fact, feel the hair on their skin rise. They began to feel "charged". And it reminded Randy of being close to a piece of equipment in the laboratory. The electricity sort of "jumped" from one place to another. And, if a "human" happened to be in the path.... The electrical current made its way into the system. That is to say, the biological system of a "person". Physiology 101, the basic elements of the human system.... so, the electricity is intrinsic to the system. A source of energy was coming from what looked like a "reactor". This piece of equipment did not have a significant impact on the physiology of Rebecca, Randy and Tina. But, they did feel something. It was a "sensation", a warmth within and underneath their skin.... And as Tina got close to Randy, she "zapped" him. They laughed. It was "static electricity"! curious thing? Physics in this world.... But, wasn't it more? Randy reflected on a time he had been doing physical training aboard a Navy ship. Running along different areas of the ship, topside and below deck, he took a turn into a corridor that led down a flight of steps... which, he followed into an area that was "electrically charged". The area was "tagged off". That is, a way to mark that the system needed a warning of severe electrical charges. Good to know, when floating in and surrounded by nothing but ocean! Electricity doesn't "ground-well" in that sort of circumstance. He quickly turned around and got away from the "tagged out" area.... He smiled as he reflected and rubbed his arm, where Tina had just "zapped" him with her electricity. So, it was more though.... Wasn't it? The cells within the human body. The tissues, which were groups of likable cells. The organs.... A higher level of cells; grouped to function in a higher level task.... Like respiration in the human lung! What powered all of it? electricity! The biologists called it "action potentials". Fascinating, really it was.... It is.... The fact that "electricity" could travel along designated internal human system paths.... Along complicated "efficient lines" that were, at times, bundled with "insulation"! And, more interesting, gaps in some the pathways where "chemical signals" were efficiently utilized. Similar to a message along two paper cups and a long string, between! What was that chemical (Randy thought)? Acetylcholine... he smiled. Tina nudged him because she knew he was temporarily lost in the "thinking process". And she followed her nudge with a hug and kiss. They smiled at each other. Because they were connected in more efficient ways... even more efficient than electricity.... The tethers of the soul. They were, they are soul mates....

The reactor hummed and then a large flash of light was released into the surrounding area. Something was happening in this lab. Something that Rebecca believed was connected to the University basement furnace.... "the system" which fueled "this place", "this time" ... They needed to confront the evil that guarded that furnace.... And it would happen very soon.... Rebecca had been in this place, in this time – wherever this place and time brought her.... for a very long time. She knew of the furnace, of the evil guard dogs.... Of the evil engineer that feed the furnace with the souls of innocent victims.... She prepared Tina and Randy. She explained that what was needed to stop this entity was found in her bag. The bag she brought from "China Town". Inside this bag was some very important tools. A cross. Not anything ordinary, though. It was blessed and it was antique. She really did not know, for sure, where it came from. It was from ancient times and it was very powerful. That was the tool to destroy the evil engineer. They needed to place it on or near his heart. Where his "heart" should be. Rebecca believed that there was something more in the order of black sludge, in place of healthy functioning cardiac muscle. Who really knew? Perhaps, there was no electro physiology in the evil entities "heart". He was a walking dead. As were others, in his crew.... For the dogs...... they had something more ninja like! Sort of like Chinese stars. They were bad-ass. Sharp as hell, and with a bright silver shine. No ordinary silver. Something blessed. A glow of fluorescence at each star tip. That would be used to take out the dogs and any goons that were in the basement.... And, finally – they would need to get to the hot furnace. With holy water... that was contained in a special flask, they would throw it into the fire. This "water" was also not ordinary. The contents were something out of this world. The concentration was suspected to be something fierce.... The water glowed a very bright yellow – a steady glow.... To bright to look directly at, for long... They were now on their way, walking across campus to the science building. At the very bottom, in the basement - they found the evil engineer, surrounded by his goons and attack dover dogs.

Randy and Tina took charge of the "interference". While Rebecca went after the evil engineer. The dogs were vicious! Attacking at Randy's ankles, then snapping at Tina's face! The silver stars were whipped into the air, and as they travelled through the extremely hot mist – the glow zig zagged.... Pointing directly at and landing straight into the throat of each beast. The "blessed" stars destroyed each animal and were used to melt the remaining "walking dead". As the fight continued, the flame inside the furnace diminished.... Tina threw her last star at the engineer, barely missing Rebecca. The combination of star glow and holy water absolutely dissolved the evil entity, before their very eyes. Almost, like a melting ice cream cone. He was gone. The furnace roared in defiance. Rebecca opened the door and threw the blessed water into the fire. Immediately, a flash of soft blue light emanated out of the furnace – through the room! It was a cool light... that instantly removed the terrible heat. Tina led Randy and Rebecca out of the basement and back to ground level. They hugged and rejoiced... they destroyed the evil that was holding this place and time "hostage" ... and, as they looked around – the environment seemed "lighter", "brighter" ...The group walked back to the main part of the University campus, then sat down. It had been exhausting to deal with such evil, to even be a part of such a dark entity. But, they did it and now they were resting. Just, resting.... As they sat in a nice part of the University, where people walked around them.... There was something very different. These "people" were now walking with what seemed to be a re-defined "purpose". They were, in fact, going somewhere.... and Rebecca suspected that although the furnace had been destroyed, although the evil gate keepers of the furnace were destroyed, and although the evil guard dogs of the furnace with goons, had been destroyed…. There was now a cool energy supporting this place and time. That "energy" was emanating from the lab. Rebecca remembered that when they were there, looking around…. There was some kind of transport capability. So, they talked and after some time…. agreed to return to that energy. Perhaps, just perhaps, it would be possible to return Randy and Tina to their University. Rebecca wanted to go with them….

The End